Bats Out of Hell

VIKINGS ROCK!
Book 1

by Lily Harlem

"Sex, Drugs, & Rock 'n' Row

© Copyright 2025 by Lily Harlem
Text by Lily Harlem
Cover by Dar Albert

Dragonblade Publishing, Inc. is an imprint of Kathryn Le Veque Novels, Inc.
P.O. Box 23
Moreno Valley, CA 92556
ceo@dragonbladepublishing.com

Produced in the United States of America

First Edition April 2025
Print Edition

Reproduction of any kind except where it pertains to short quotes in relation to advertising or promotion is strictly prohibited.

All Rights Reserved.

The characters and events portrayed in this book are fictitious. Any similarity to real persons, living or dead, is purely coincidental and not intended by the author.

ARE YOU SIGNED UP FOR DRAGONBLADE'S BLOG?

You'll get the latest news and information on exclusive giveaways, exclusive excerpts, coming releases, sales, free books, cover reveals and more.

Check out our complete list of authors, too!

No spam, no junk. That's a promise!

Sign Up Here

www.dragonbladepublishing.com

Dearest Reader;

Thank you for your support of a small press. At Dragonblade Publishing, we strive to bring you the highest quality Historical Romance from some of the best authors in the business. Without your support, there is no 'us', so we sincerely hope you adore these stories and find some new favorite authors along the way.

Happy Reading!

CEO, Dragonblade Publishing

Additional Dragonblade books by
Author Lily Harlem

VIKINGS ROCK!
Bats Out of Hell (Book 1)

Hawk Castle Series
Loved by the Last Knight (Book 1)
Adored by the Archduke (Book 2)
Embraced by the Emperor (Book 3)

The Lyon's Den Series
Lyon at the Altar

Chapter One

KING URD STOOD still and silent in the leafy shade of Yggdrasil, a divine tree so ancient and sacred, the top branches reached another realm. He closed his eyes and blew out a misty breath. He was not a young man and the cold and rugged journey to Uppsala had made his bones weary and his feet ache.

And with each step, he'd been reminded that he would be feasting with the gods before too long.

Which presented him with a problem.

Four problems, to be precise. A number that didn't bode well. Three, six, or nine problems, he could handle. Four, that was a number tainted with misfortune and dispute. Something his wily, headstrong offspring had more than enough of already.

A goat bleated to his right, one of nine males awaiting sacrifice. A rooster joined in the animal chatter as if rejoicing in their shared fate. Tomorrow, their blood would be basted on Yggdrasil's trunk and branches, an offering to the gods to both appease and revere them.

Urd sighed and rubbed his temples. If only Orm had volunteered all those years ago to be one of the nine young human males to be sacrificed, he would only have three children to contend with. But Orm hadn't been ready to drink with Odin, Thor, and Freya back then. He'd said he'd had battles to win and journeys to make. He'd wanted to wait for a Valkyrie to escort him to Valhalla. It had been an angry conversation, as proffering himself to the gods would have been a great honor for the family, even though Urd's wife, Inga—long gone now—hadn't wanted it, either.

"Father! Finally. I've been searching high and low for you."

Urd opened his eyes at the sound of his daughter's voice. He turned, using his wooden cane to support his weak left leg. "I am sure you did not search long, Astrid."

"I wondered if you'd gone to the temple ahead of the festival. Thor is as demanding as ever and needs to be placated." She rolled her eyes. "He must be worshipped and adored if we are not to starve half to death next summer."

"It is true the crops were poor. But Thor will be well honored in due course."

Astrid flicked her scarlet hair over her shoulders. She'd worn it in long plaits for the journey and they hung like ropes down to her waist.

"The crops last year were awful, Father. If it happens again, there will be famine for your people."

Urd nodded slowly. "The sea will provide."

"Only if the gods are kind. Andhrímnir demands sacrifices and devotion too."

"The divine chef will provide the way he provides for the gods each day in Valhalla."

"I hope so." She took his hand and squeezed.

Her skin was warm and soft, though she had a long, silvery scar that ran down her right forearm to her knuckles, the result of a close call with a sword during a battle south of Drangar.

"But I trust you, Father," she went on, "for you're our king, and luckily, you have a good brain in your skull."

"You are kind to me."

"To you, yes, because I love you. My enemies, hah, I am the opposite of kind." She laughed, a high-pitched sound that sent a foraging bird into the air with a squawk. "Come on. Let's find Haakon and Ravn."

"Where are they?" Urd walked with her, his heavy, wolf-skin robe brushing against the frozen forest floor.

"Ravn is helping prepare the golden chain. Haakon, I haven't seen for a while."

"And Orm? Where is he?"

"He still hasn't arrived." Weak midwinter light pierced the canopy, slicing over her petite features and flashing on the golden brooch—the image of a wolf's head—that pinned her cloak into place.

"He should have been here yesterday." Urd couldn't keep the annoyance from his voice. "Why he didn't leave Drangar with us, I don't know."

"I've asked Joseph to let us know the moment he rides in—"

"And ride, he will. The boy has no decency. He should walk. Every nine years, it is a mark of respect to the gods to walk to Uppsala."

"Oh, don't think about that. He'll be here soon and that's what matters. Then you'll have all your delightful children together for the great festival."

Urd's lips twisted and he stopped himself from muttering further frustrations about his youngest son, who seemed to purposefully go out of his way to anger him.

"Fuck me, look, there's amanita." Astrid pointed at a crop of tiny, red fungi growing in a warm crack in a tree trunk.

"Astrid, language."

"Sorry, but you can't deny they'll be useful for the sacrifices."

He sighed. "*Ja*, they will and you have a good eye. We will gather them and take them to Hildi. She will prepare them."

Astrid plucked the small mushrooms, putting them into a tattered, leather purse.

Urd waited patiently and studied the concentration on her pretty face. She was a good daughter. Fiery, it was true, but that just made her a better warrior. She was an accomplished shield-maiden, just like her mother had been. A fighter you wanted at your side in battle. One who didn't shy away because someone was bigger or shouted louder.

Instead, she used her nimble, lightweight body to dodge and then deliver deathly blows when they were least expected.

He would have liked to pass on his royal title to her, seeing that she was older than the twins and bright of mind, but he knew neither Haakon nor Ravn would tolerate that. In their eyes, Drangar had to have a king—a king with *their* chosen queen on the throne next to them.

But which twin should it be?

The twins were his biggest two problems. Two. Another number he didn't like.

Astrid finished plucking the precious crop and stood. She straightened Urd's cape as though worried the winter chill was nipping the wrinkled skin of his neck.

"There is rabbit broth in the pot. You should eat soon," she said. "You must keep up your strength."

"I could eat." He flexed and unflexed his free hand, the one not holding the cane. "And the heat of a fire would be most welcome."

They walked in silence, navigating a frozen stream with icy stepping stones that poked from the ground-level mist. A fallen branch blocked the path and Astrid hacked at it with a bone-handled axe she'd pulled from her belt, her breaths puffing in front of her face.

Soon, the sounds and smells of the camp filtered toward them. Urd's belly rumbled and his mouth watered in anticipation of the rich, herby broth awaiting him.

To the left of his *tjald*—a material structure that mimicked his longhouse back at Drangar—he saw a group of children sitting around a fire with threads of black smoke licking up to the canopy. They were silent, enraptured, and wide eyed.

Urd saw why and stopped.

His son Haakon was speaking to them. He was leaning forward, gesturing, his features animated.

"He is regaling them with sagas," Astrid said quietly.

"Let us listen."

"But, Father, you are tired and hungry and—"

"Do not fuss over your king," Urd snapped. "I once went two weeks without food and water and then killed a bear with my own hands, no weapon, as you well know."

Astrid was quiet for a moment. "I will tell Joseph you're here." She stepped away, disturbing a branch heavy with snow. The tiny flakes fluttered in the breeze, sparkling in the torchlight as they danced.

Urd took a step closer to his son and the beguiled children.

"The Norns will sit beneath the leaves of Yggdrasil, which, as you know, is just yonder, and spin their terrible fates. There will be so many Norns, too many to count, and their power is fantastic, unstoppable, and laced with evil." Haakon paused and looked around at his audience. He leaned further forward. "I wish not to scare you children, but you should know how the end of the world, the end of even the gods, will come about."

Urd gripped the bear's head carved into the top of his cane and waited for the story he knew well to continue.

"A great winter will come, the wind so bitter, it takes the skin from cheeks. The sun will fade in the sky, its heat gone. The winter will be endless, the summer no more. Crops will fail, people will starve, people will kill each other for what little there is left. There will be no laws, no jarls, no kings. Can you imagine that?" Again, he paused. "The wolves Skoll and Hait, who have hunted the sun and the moon in the skies since the beginning of time, will at last catch their prey. They will gobble up the stars too. Everything will be black. Our great tree Yggdrasil will shake and shiver, causing all the other trees, the cliffs, and the mountains to fall flat to the ground." He spoke quickly. "The chain that has been holding back the evil wolf Fenrir will break, and the monstrous beast will run free. The mighty serpent Jormungand, who dwells at the very bottom of the ocean and encircles the land holding his tail in his mouth, will rise from the depths, no longer holding his charge and spilling the seas over all the earth as he makes landfall."

Urd blew out a breath, the story so familiar, yet hearing it from his son's mouth and with such passion had his heart rate picking up and his nerves tingling. What a terrifying day it would be.

"Naglfar will be shaken free from its moorings. A wicked ship made from the fingernails and toenails of dead men, women, and children. It will sail the flooded earth, taking its terrifying crew of giants and the captain with it. And who is the captain? I will tell you." He held up his finger. "It is Loki, the traitor to the gods. Yes, that's right, the traitor Loki is captain of Naglfar."

The children gasped and looked at each other.

"The end of the world continues," Haakon boomed. "The wolf Fenrir will run over the earth, mouth open and scooping everything up and eating it. The serpent Jormungand will spit his poisonous venom over land, into the sea, and through the air. The sky will split and the fire-giants with their flaming swords will march to the home of the gods, Asgard, and as the sentry horns blast out, the gods will know they must gather their swords and shields and go to battle."

"My son can certainly paint a story—the gods gave him that," Urd said as his stomach rumbled again. He glanced at his tent with smoke dancing from its roof opening and wiped away snowflakes from his eyelashes. He'd leave Haakon to his sagas and go and eat.

"Ravn, I thought you were at the temple hanging the golden chains?" Urd said, ducking into the warmth and stamping snow from his boots.

Ravn looked up from where he was hunched over his bowl of steaming stew. His blue eyes were piercing in the firelight and the metal beads and charms hanging from the end of his thick, black beard flashed. "*Ja*, I was." He shoveled in more food. "But now I'm here."

"And Siggy? She is here?"

Ravn picked up a wooden tankard and took a slug of mead. "Aye, she's with her mother."

"Good. At least that means only Orm is late." Urd clicked his tongue on the roof of his mouth.

Ravn chewed on bread. "Siggy is with child again."

"She is?" Urd sat next to his son and held his hands to a fire trough. "I congratulate you. You are indeed blessed by the gods. She gave you a son just last year."

"I offer my thanks daily." His voice was gruff.

Ravn was tired. Hungry too, judging by the way he was spooning in food. He always had been a grump when weary with an empty stomach.

"Here, Father. Eat this up." Astrid placed a bowl of broth in his hands. A large hunk of bread sat within it, already soaking up the juice.

"Thank you, Astrid."

She smiled at him and placed a tankard of mead on the bench at his side. "Anything for the king. It's a big day tomorrow."

"Indeed, it is." The broth was rich and salty and warmed his gullet. "Did you see Orm?"

Ravn shook his head.

Urd sighed. "I will be most displeased with him if he is late."

Ravn huffed and finished his drink. He held it up for Joseph to refill. "You're always pissed with him about something."

Urd said nothing.

"But what does it matter if he doesn't turn up?" Ravn went on with a flippant wave. "He's nothing more than an embarrassment, the runt of the litter. For I can provide you with heirs even if none of your other sons can."

"It is true." Urd nodded slowly. "I am sure your boy, Thormod, will grow to be a fine man."

"He is just a bairn; the other not even born yet." Astrid sat on the opposite side of the fire trough with her food. She raised her eyebrows at Ravn. "Don't count your chickens before they hatch."

"*Ja*, but I have my reign to live out before my sons take over. Plenty of time for fucking and for Siggy to give me many more children." He chuckled. "And they will all grow to become fine men and strong warriors. Didn't your rune stones tell me that, Astrid?"

"Ha, you presume you will be king. How bold, dear brother." Haakon's voice suddenly filled the tent. "When we are twins."

He filled the entrance, snow peppering his black, furred cape and his narrowed eyes flashing. He pushed at his hood and scraped a hand through his long, dark hair. Around his neck, a boar's fang hung on a length of leather and he'd shaved his facial hair in preparation for the festival, revealing the intricate tattoo that ran from his jawline down to his throat.

"Being born on the same day does not mean we are equal." Ravn sat up straighter.

"Sure, it does." Haakon strode over to Astrid and set his hands on her shoulders. He leaned over and kissed her on the top of her head. "Sister, I am glad you have arrived. And you're looking sensational, as always."

"It is good to see you, brother. Are you well?"

"I need food."

"For you." Thrall Joseph offered Haakon a bowl of stew.

"Ah, great. And a drink. I have been telling sagas to the children. I am dry as a bone. The little ankle biters wouldn't let me go." He chuckled.

Urd watched his son sit and tuck into his broth. He was as tall and broad as Ravn, but he sat straighter and he seemed more alert to what was going on around him. His attention flicked from his sister to Ravn, the servants, and the doorway. He glanced at the beds that had been set up for the royal family and surveyed the food store. He was a sponge, always curious, always seeking to understand.

Both twins were fierce and skilled fighters. They'd been to battle more times than Urd could count and each time, the gods had been kind. But Urd saw in Haakon a softer, more thoughtful streak. Ravn wouldn't take the time to tell sagas, not even to his own child, yet Haakon sought out a young audience. Ravn was short-tempered with his sister, yet Haakon understood her complex moods and knew flattery got him in her good books every time.

These thoughts swirled in Urd's mind. Which temperament would make for the better king? He should make a decision. Choose. And that would be the end of it.

He sighed and sat back. His spine creaked and he groaned softly.

"Are you unwell, Father?" Haakon asked.

"No. Just tired." He smiled at his son. "I will sleep soon."

"You've hardly touched your food. Eat more," Astrid said, gesturing to his bowl with her spoon. "You'll get sick."

"Do not mother me, girl." He raised his eyebrows at her, though a smile tickled his lips. "For I am your king."

"And you would not let us forget it," she said with a laugh. "Oh, High and Mighty One. Must we bow to you constantly?"

"Do not tease your king, Astrid." Haakon chuckled and picked up his drink. "Where is Orm?" He took a gulp. "Or shouldn't I ask?"

Chapter Two

HAAKON STUDIED HIS father as they walked past the sacred grove and toward the majestic temple of Uppsala. Huge, shiny, golden chains had been looped over and around branches and could be seen for miles, guiding worshipers to the hills, where the nine days of festivities would be held.

Haakon worried about the stoop in the king's back and the way his left leg dragged a little. Part of the worry was that he knew how much it must have frustrated his father for his body to be fading. He'd been such a strong, vibrant, brave warrior, a tireless and intelligent leader of people, and a seafarer with such skill and knowledge, his name would be on the tongue of many for years to come.

But fading he was and soon, either Haakon or Ravn would be chosen as his successor. Unless, of course, the king opted for Astrid, which wouldn't be a ridiculous idea. She was a renowned shield-maiden, smart and brave, and she would take the responsibility seriously.

But did she have the respect of the people of Drangar and surrounding providences? That, Haakon wasn't sure about. There were times she hadn't endeared herself to them with her fiery nature and sharp tongue.

"If Orm has not arrived and is not already waiting for us..." Urd said a little breathlessly. "I will disown him. He will be no son of mine."

"He'll be here," Haakon said, beating down a wave of anger at his younger brother. This was not what his father needed today.

"He disrespects me," Urd went on. "With his foolish ways and his fanciful ideas. It is as if has no notion he is the son of a king. He makes me ashamed and shows others I have little control over my own family."

"He knows he is your son, Father, and what that means. I am sure of it. And I am sure he will not bring shame on this, our most hallowed of days."

Urd huffed.

They passed the sacred grove containing Yggdrasil, its branches empty now, though soon today's sacrificed bodies, three in total, one man and two animals, would be hoisted up there.

The ice had melted a little around the stepping stones, and Haakon steadied his father as they crossed.

"Not far now."

Urd paused. He pulled in a breath.

At the end of a winding, shadowed path, through the haunting, winter mist, the temple came into view. Tall, wooden pillars supported the staved, sloping roofs and freshly swept steps led to a huge polished doorway. The forest had encroached over the last nine years and had now been hacked back by the *gothi*—silent holy men—leaving splintered saplings and torn ivy tendrils.

The door was closed, awaiting the king to open it and in doing so start the festivities.

The gathered crowd spotted the king and the hum of conversation quieted.

"Your people await," Haakon said, adjusting the steel arm ring that coiled around his left bicep. It had been a gift from his father to celebrate him reaching manhood at his fifteen summers.

Ravn was at the top of the steps, near the temple door. Haakon frowned. The king had to enter the temple first on this special day. It should be no one else.

Yet Ravn, wearing a white, furred cape complete with heavy amber and silver pendants, stood feet apart, arms crossed, and chin tilted, as though he already thought himself king.

The blood heated in Haakon's veins, searing around his body and making his skin itch. He could have rushed ahead that morning and harnessed the crowd's attention, made himself comfortable in the position of the next king of Drangar's lands. But he hadn't. He'd chosen to walk with his father, ensure he arrived safely, that each step was sure and steady and his fractious mood was placated.

As they passed through the crowd and neared the temple, Haakon caught Ravn's gaze.

Triumph seemed to flash in his brother's eyes and he tilted his chin a little more. He noticeably glanced at their father's silver crown, as though sizing it up. Of all the nerve.

Haakon tensed his jaw and spotted Astrid. She'd released her hair and it flowed around her shoulders like a river of molten rock, the weak sunlight glinting off it. She wore a thick, green, woolen gown with buckled leather details at the waist, shoulders, and wrists. Despite her small stature, she looked every bit the formidable fighter and combined with being a beautiful princess, she was indeed a force that many men found too much to handle.

Haakon was grateful she was his sister so she could never be his wife. Her husband would need to be a braver man than he and he'd yet to meet such a person.

"Ah, there is Ravn," Urd said, nodding forward. "Awaiting, as he should be."

Haakon bit back a retort and instead said, "And Astrid is here."

"So still one missing." Urd grunted and his eyes narrowed.

Suddenly, there was a shuffling in the crowd. People parted, unleashing a flurry of movement and exclamations.

"Father! Do not fear, I am here!" Orm landed in front of them, as though he'd sprung frog-like from the gathering crowd. He stood with arms outstretched, a broad grin on his face and black kohl swiped thickly beneath his eyes—the damp weather having made it bleed down his cheeks like tears.

"Orm!" Urd stopped suddenly. "Where in Odin's name have you just come from?"

"From Drangar, Father. You know that." In his other hand, Orm held up a long string of animal bones that he shook noisily at Haakon. "Brother, I see you have taken on the role of nursemaid to the king." He laughed, a brittle, deep cackle. "Keep up the good work." Orm winked at his father, a cheeky gesture that only a youngest son would dare produce. "Where is my favorite sister?"

He spun around and upon seeing Astrid, he scooped her up and swung her in a full circle, the string of bones gliding outward the way her legs did.

"Orm!" She clipped him around the head. "Be somber, for we are here to start a ceremony honoring the gods. We do not wish them to think we are flippant."

"*Ja, ja,* of course." Orm set her down. He then straightened his tunic, attached the bones to his belt, and pulled his mouth into a flat line. "The gods, they await their sacrifices. We must be very somber, indeed." He nodded slowly.

Despite Orm's words, Haakon knew his brother wasn't being as respectful as he should have been. He treated so many things as a jest. Important, serious things that made both Haakon and Astrid worried for Orm's success in reaching Valhalla. If he displeased the gods, he'd be denied entry, or given thrall's work, nothing more than a slave, for all eternity.

Urd carried on walking, nodding at the crowd as he went. Their outstretched hands stroked the fur of his cape for good fortune. Many had traveled from outlying villages and rarely saw their king. His presence was as important to them as the worshipping of the gods, for they saw him as their protector as well as ruler.

He passed the *gothi*, who stood with their long, dark capes brushing the ground. Each man held steel bowls they'd later use for blood collecting. Their lips were basted in dark kohl, reminding worshippers they never spoke. Their ears were also blackened, as were their eyelids.

Haakon helped his father up the steps to the temple door. Astrid and Orm stayed close behind, their footsteps heavy on the wood. The scent of sage burning in four large torches filled Haakon's nose. Beneath his feet were scattered, crushed acorns.

Urd turned to the crowd, then, after passing his cane to Astrid, held up his arms. "People of our lands, I, King Urd of Rhalson, welcome you to this sacred festival in Uppsala. Over the next nine days, we will honor Odin, Thor, and Freya. We will appease their rage and promise our loyalty. We will give blood to save blood. We offer food as we ourselves feast because our fare is too lowly for the gods. We will dance and celebrate our good fortune at having such wise, powerful, strong gods." He paused and looked at the sea of faces. "Now let us begin with the opening of the temple door and allow the pale Yule light to penetrate the home of the gods here on land and soil."

Astrid passed him his cane, and again, he turned.

But before he could reach the heavy, brass latch and open the temple door, Ravn stepped before it, and with a quick twist of his wrist, he threw the door open. "Most revered gods, your servants arrive with gifts and worship," Ravn bellowed, stealing the words that should have come from Urd's mouth.

Rage flooded Haakon. He pushed forward and grabbed his brother's shoulder before he could take the first step into the temple. He shoved him—hard. "How dare you?"

Ravn staggered to the right, clearly taken by surprise. Then he turned to Haakon, fists clenched and eyes narrowed. "What the—?"

In a fit of temper, Haakon delivered a punch to Ravn's jaw, snapping his head back and causing him to bump into a flaming torch. Sparks flew into the air as Astrid lunged to steady it. Acorns scattered.

"You dare to open the temple door on this day?!" Haakon shouted, getting his face right in and close to his brother's. "You dare to presume that is *your* right?"

"It *is* my fucking right." A drip of blood swelled on Ravn's lower lip. "I am the king's son." His eyes flashed with pride and stubbornness.

"As am I, and I do not consider it my right to open this door until our father is feasting with the gods. Until then, I wait. I respect." Haakon snarled and gritted his teeth. "I do not presume."

"Then you will lose, brother."

"Lose what?"

"The crown." Ravn shoved him—hard—with his palms flat on Haakon's chest, as though dismissing him, pushing him away from sight and thought—pushing him to somewhere Haakon couldn't be seen or heard.

This just made Haakon more furious and he pulled out his freshly sharpened dagger. "We might have grown in our mother's belly at the same time, Ravn, but that will not stop me from killing you."

"You couldn't if you tried for one hundred years!" Anger had deepened his voice.

"*Ja*. Kill him, Haakon," Astrid snapped. "His plan is to usurp us all." She withdrew an iron spear and a feral wildness flashed in her eyes. "If you do not, Haakon, I bloody well will."

"Such drama!" Orm said, passing between them and clapping as though thoroughly entertained. "And I thought spectacle-making was my domain."

"Get out of here, Orm," Ravn snapped.

"Leave? Just when things are getting interesting?" He poked Ravn's shoulder. "What are you going to do, huh? Kill our brother and sister? And then me and our father? Just so you can place the crown upon your head?"

Ravn growled and slid his sword from its sheath. He held it up, the dangerously sharp point only a few feet from Haakon's face.

Orm laughed.

Astrid spat on the floor and widened her stance. "Go on, Ravn, try it."

"Enough!" Urd slammed his cane on the wooden boards. "Do not anger the gods this way!"

Haakon was suddenly aware of the still silence that had fallen over the crowd. All eyes were on them. And they were wide, scared eyes. To be drawing weapons against kin on the holy temple steps was indeed a sight to behold. And it would not be one that was forgotten if the crops failed, if storms shattered boats in the harbor, if wolves and bears took bairns from their cribs. The siblings would be blamed for angering the gods by disrespecting them in their home.

"Father." Astrid blew out a breath. She closed her eyes for a second and when she opened them, the flash of crazy Haakon had seen before had gone. "Forgive us."

"Step aside," Urd said roughly as he elbowed forward, ignoring the weapons held aloft around him. "I will not be party to your immature squabbles and you should stop humiliating yourselves."

"'Immature squabbles'?" Astrid snapped. "Ravn is trying to claim a throne that is not his to claim."

"Who says it is not mine?" Ravn said, swiping at the drip of blood rolling from his lip and onto his beard.

"Me!" Haakon growled. "The throne is as much mine as it is yours. No one knows which one of us was born first, remember."

"It was me. I was born first." Ravn stabbed his thumb against his chest.

"Says who?"

"I know it in my heart."

"Your heart deceives you."

"Stop!" Urd said, his back to them. "Or I will order the *gothi* to sacrifice you all to the gods on this very day just so I can have some peace."

Haakon clamped his lips shut. He had no intention of being sacrificed, no matter how much of an honor it was. He still had battles to win, a crown to claim, heirs to produce.

"Good," Urd said, taking the silence as compliance with his command. "Now let us pay our respects."

He stepped into the temple and the *gothi* quickly followed him, sweeping past Haakon, Ravn, Astrid, and Orm as though they were floating.

A chanter woman, her face streaked with red, began her soulful song, the dulcet tune winding around the bare branches of the forest like trickling honey.

Re-sheathing his sword, Ravn stepped close to Haakon and in a low voice said, "Make no mistake, brother, I will wear that crown and I am prepared to fight you to the death for it."

"I do not doubt it, for I see the wolf-like hunger for power in your eyes," Haakon said. "But remember, my blood is your blood, my bone is your bone. If ever there was a fair match, it is between you and I. You cannot predict the outcome when we have been raised as one."

Astrid suddenly pushed between them. She spoke in a harsh whisper and wagged her finger. "When we return to Drangar, we will call an assembly. We will decide once and for all upon this matter."

"An assembly," Haakon said, not taking his attention from Ravn. "No, my brother has declared he will fight to the death for our father's crown and that is what we will do. When we have completed our nine days of honoring the gods and feasting in Uppsala, we will fight it out…to the death. That, dear sister, is the only way we will solve the matter of who is to be the next king."

Chapter Three

KENNA GATHERED UP her heavy, woolen skirt and ran as though her life depended upon it. Truth was, her life *did* depend upon it!

Angering a mother boar had not been a sensible thing to do. And anger it, she had. Kenna had killed one of its offspring and had it tucked beneath her arm. The life had gone from it, thanks to her dagger, but still, the mother wanted it back.

She pushed through a patch of brambles, devoid of leaves and fruit but still sharp with thorns. A curse tore from her throat as she heard the ripping of material. Her mother would not be happy.

But her mother would be happy at the thought of a suckling this time of year. The sow had given birth late summer, the sun dipping in the sky. Not sensible when all around there were hungry humans and ravenous wolves. She'd be surprised if any of the litter survived to see the first snowdrop.

With a glance over her shoulder, Kenna took a track to her left, relying on the fact the mother boar had terrible eyesight and would run straight ahead. Well, until the scent of her offspring petered out, that was. Then she'd turn and come searching this way.

A pheasant took flight, releasing a shrill alarm call. It disturbed a branch laden with snow, which fell to the ground with a *whump*, just missing Kenna. She was breathing hard, her legs pounding. She couldn't outrun the boar; she'd have to outwit it.

She threw a quick glance behind her, her hair whipping across her face. The boarlet was heavy, which was good for cooking, but not for carrying. She took another turn, toward the river. She'd cross it and her trail would disappear. She just had to get there.

Kenna could still hear the huge beast, grunting, snorting and its trotters thumping the earth. How far from its nest would it go?

On and on she ran. The boar was getting more distant now, but also more frantic. She could hear it crashing through the undergrowth, gnashing and squealing. The creature was clearly murderous, her maternal instinct well and truly activated.

The scent of the icy river filled Kenna's nostrils, and she shifted her catch from one arm to the other, blood smearing over her gown.

To her right, she spotted wolf tracks and a shudder went through her. She hated wolves. A close call when she'd been checking traps with Hamish, years ago, had given her nightmares for an entire winter. But today, she didn't have time to fear the wolf. For today, she'd been the predator and she had her prey.

The river was a bubbling mass of mountain water this time of year, but it wasn't deep on this bend because it meandered unusually wide. So, gathering her gown higher, she began to wade. It wasn't easy with already tired legs, but she forged forward, still occasionally glancing behind and praying to God she wouldn't see the fierce face and glinting eyes of a wild boar.

At one point, she nearly dropped her treasure but quickly righted herself and stepped over the rock that had almost twisted her ankle. Soon, she reached the opposite bank. It was hard with frost and she threw the boarlet to the grass then heaved herself up using roots as handholds. Even if the boar did follow her now, it would never be able to climb the steep incline.

Finally, she stood, hands on hips, kill at her feet, and dragged-in breath. She'd made it. Home was not far from here. Her daring had paid off. Her kin would feast tonight and for many nights to come.

"Ah!" she said, bending forward at the waist and peering across the river. "There you are."

She spied the boar that had been chasing her, but it couldn't see her as it pushed under a fallen branch and pile of leaves on the other side of the river. It had been a close call, that was for sure. The boar would have happily mauled her as retribution.

"I am sorry," Kenna said, "for taking from you, but God has provided and we must eat, as must you."

The boar froze; its hearing was excellent. It turned its head, but not in Kenna's direction. The rush of water was distorting sound.

She decided not to push her luck. The river had shallow banks farther downstream and if the boar was determined enough, she might continue her pursuit. Which wouldn't be wise, as it had three other boarlets to care for that were currently at the mercy of whatever other beasts were roaming.

So Kenna stooped, sweat peppering her brow, and picked up her dinner. Within seconds, she'd slipped into the forest and onto a track she knew as well as the back of her hand.

The sun was sliding from the sky and golden shadows stretched like fingers over the frozen earth. She sped up when she'd reached the rock she and Hamish had played on as kids, not wanting to be out in the dark with only a dagger and smelling like a three-course meal to any passing wolf.

Soon, Tillicoulty, a small, wooden fortified village perched upon a hill, came into view. Home. Always had been and always would be. Torches were set on either side of the one entrance and a villager stood on the watchtower above it. Smoke rose from many dwellings, including from the chimney of the Great House at the center. And a black flag depicting the red images of a horse hoof and a fish flapped in the easterly wind.

She drew nearer. A dog barked. An ironmonger hammered.

"What you got there, Kenna?"

Bryce, tall and dark-haired, approached, pushing at his tasseled hood. He held an axe; likely, he'd been chopping firewood.

She grinned and held up the boarlet. "Dinner. Taken fresh just minutes ago."

"'Fresh'? You find a farrowing nest?"

"Aye, on the yonder side of the river. Like taking a blanket from a bairn." She laughed.

"And the mother?"

"She was nearby." Kenna shrugged, trying to feign nonchalance for the daring act she'd committed.

He shook his head. "Bit bloody risky." His attention drifted down to her toes and back up again. "And it looks like she caught you."

"Ha, you think I'd be here to tell the tale if she had?" She brushed at her dirty, wet gown. "I'm skilled in hunting. She didn't catch me, much as she wanted to."

He examined the animal. "It's a good size. Want me to carry it?"

"No, I've made it this far." She stepped around him. "I'm taking it to my mother. She'll be pleased."

"As will the *toísech*."

"Aye, my father has a fondness for suckling." She almost skipped away, renewed energy in her step despite her big chase. It was good to remind the young men of the village that women could also hunt, run, and outwit dangerous beasts. They spent their time puffing up their chests, firing arrows, and setting traps, yet she could do all of those things and more.

"Mother, look what I have for you." She entered their roundhouse, pausing for a moment for her eyes to adjust to the low light of the tallow candles.

"In heaven's name, Kenna, what have you done to your gown?" She wiped her hands on her own pale-green gown and then tucked her long, graying hair over her ears.

"Oh...aye, that. Sorry. But here. Look." She held forward the boarlet. "We will eat well tonight."

Her mother's expression, cast in shadows, went from extreme

irritation to delight and then flushed with anger. "Dear Lord above, where have you been all alone to find such a thing?"

"Over the river, toward the coast."

"*Toward the coast!* I told you not to go there. Norsemen have been spotted in the distance, on their longboats. Can you imagine if they landed on our shores and found a beautiful young woman like you?" She paused, shuddered, then crossed herself. "They are heathens, with no morals, no faith, and no conscience." She took the boar. "Just wait until your father hears about this."

"Until I hear about what?"

Kenna turned at the sound of her father's deep voice. He'd stepped into their home with Hamish at his side. Hamish was taller than her father now, having had a growth spurt during the summer.

"Your daughter, Noah, has been over the river, alone, without even telling me where she was going."

"You wouldn't have let me go," Kenna said, frustrated that the spoils of her bravery were not being admired.

"Of course I wouldn't't've." Her mother slapped the boarlet onto a wooden table and picked up a seax: a long, steel knife with a fat, wooden handle.

"It's too dangerous," her father said, "and you are the daughter of the *toísech*, you must set an example for the other young women in the village. Show them the way."

"*Show them the way.*" Kenna slammed her bloody hands on her hips. "I *am* showing them the way. The way to be strong and independent. To fend for themselves, feed themselves, and—"

"I saw wolf tracks on the other side of the river," Hamish said, folding his arms and rocking back on his heels the way her father did when asserting authority.

"Wolf tracks? Oh, Lord, give me strength." Her mother hacked more furiously at a leg.

"Did you see any wolf tracks, Kenna?" Noah asked. "Today?"

She shook her head. "Absolutely not. I would have come straight home if I had." Which was kind of the truth. She had run for home when she'd seen wolf tracks on the other side of the river.

Hamish cocked his head and she glared at him, daring her brother to question her. Though in truth he knew her better than anyone and likely knew she was fibbing.

Her father sighed. "Well, can we just agree you will not leave the village alone again?"

"Not leave the village? I can't agree to that." The thought was unbearable. She'd die of boredom.

"I didn't say not leave the village at all, I said *alone*." Noah raised his gray eyebrows at her then reached for a jug of heather ale.

"So I have to take Hamish with me every time?"

"Your brother is a fine fighter and protector, Kenna. So yes, you can go with him, or Bryce, or me, or—"

"I am also a fine fighter. I can hunt and trap and—"

"I am well aware of your skills." Her father set his hands on her shoulders. "But you are also precious and beautiful, and I am not prepared to risk harm coming to you in any shape or form. We need you here, with us, not inside the belly of a wolf or floating down an icy river." He glanced at her gown. "Which it looks like you have been doing, as you're wet through."

"Oh, dear child, go and change before the chill gets your bones," her mother said, looking up from her butchery. "And put that gown to be washed; it smells like boar dung."

Two hours later, Kenna was sitting in a clean gown tucking into a hearty meat stew laden with thyme. Her mother was still working and her father had gone to discuss village business with council.

"Mother said the Norsemen have been spotted off the coast," she said quietly to Hamish.

He nodded and wiped the back of his hand over his mouth. His green eyes flashed in the candlelight. "Twice in the last month. Their boats are so long, and they stay afloat whatever the weather, no matter how high the waves." He leaned closer. "It is as if they are a devilish magic."

"'Magic'?"

"Aye, for they navigate when the mists come in, and when the sun does not show itself? They dare to go right out to sea, whatever the weather. How do they do it?"

"I don't know." She tore at bread. "But if I ever meet one, I will ask him for you."

"I hope you never meet one. They are savages, raping and pillaging good Christians and leaving destruction in their wake." He closed his eyes and crossed himself.

Kenna had heard this many times before. "Why do you think they're like that? Surely, they have families, people they care for."

"That is exactly it. They care for no one but themselves."

"Not even God?"

He huffed. "Mother says they have no knowledge of God, but they will, on judgment day."

Kenna was quiet, wondering what it would be like to have no knowledge of God's existence. It would be strange, empty, like a gaping hole inside, like tumbling from a cliff with nothing to break the fall.

"Where do you think they're going? When they sail past Scottish shores?"

"Who knows? Ireland 'haps, the home of the missionaries, or searching for seals and whales. Maybe for Irish churches to raid."

"They wouldn't do that." Her eyes widened. "Not a church."

"They would and they have." He raised his eyebrows at her and shoveled in a spoonful of stew.

"They will get struck down, surely. For if they know not of God, they do not need his treasures." The very thought shocked and saddened her.

"Heathens take what they want. We know that much from the tales wanderers have brought with them."

Kenna was quiet for a moment, thinking about the one time she'd seen a longboat in the distance. The red, billowing sails were hoisted high and the waves being cut by a bow curled like a dragon's long neck.

Hamish set his empty bowl aside then threw a log onto the fire at the center of the room. "You must heed Father, Kenna."

"About what?"

"Going alone, out of the village. It is not safe for a girl."

"I'm twenty-one summers now. I'm a woman, and one with skills. I am perfectly fine alone."

"That might be so, but if something happened to you, it would break our family. Mother and Father would be torn in two with grief."

"And you?" She raised her eyebrows at him.

"You are infuriating and stubborn and at times sarcastic, but aye, I would miss you." He nudged her with his elbow. "So if you want to go wandering, holler at me, and I'll come with you. Or you could always ask Bryce. He'd like that."

She drank the last bit of broth from her bowl then sighed. "I will agree, for the winter at least."

"Good."

"But can we go tomorrow? To collect hazelnuts."

"What?"

"We could get samphire too, from the edge of Clam Bay."

"I have to chop logs then clean out the coop, but aye. Then we will go foraging."

"That will give me time to mend my gown." She groaned. "Mother is not happy about the damage done to it."

Chapter Four

THE CROWD AT Drangar was growing. Spreading onto the wooden piers and stony beach and circling the torches that towered in iron baskets. Longboats bobbed in the harbor, the day gray but calm.

A drum was banging repetitively. *Boom. Boom. Boom, boom, boom.*

Haakon looked at his father, who pulled his fur cape tighter and then gripped the head of his cane.

How had it come to this? It was a strange path that led to two sons fighting. Haakon's mother, Ingrid, would be watching down from her seat with the gods and shaking her head. What a waste of time, what a waste of life.

But even with that thought, Haakon would not be dissuaded. He had reveled hard during the Uppsala Festival, making much use of amanita and its ability to bring dreams to life. He had watched Ravn and his wife roll naked in the snow as though frolicking in feathers, and he himself had indulged in an orgy that had gone on for half the day and most of the night—a delicious tangle of naked, sweating bodies and uninhibited cries of pleasure.

Was he living his last days on Earth? Was that why he was so determined to live it to the maximum?

"Father. Are you ready?" Astrid asked, tightening the hood of her white fur. Her red hair peeked out of it like small, licking flames.

"Ready to watch one of my sons die? No. I will never be ready for that."

The frown on Haakon's brow deepened. He didn't want to cause his father pain but could see no way around that.

"So call a halt to it." Astrid gestured to the crowd. "You are king, Father. It's your right." She paused as a jet-black raven called from a nearby rooftop, narrowing her eyes as though trying to decipher what it was saying. "Pick one son to succeed the throne and be done with it. Both will live, even if one is unhappy."

"They would not tolerate that outcome." Urd looked at Haakon, as though hoping he might be amenable to that solution.

Haakon wasn't, so he stayed silent.

"I brought them up to be men of their word," the king went on with a sigh. "The fact that I did that is my burden to bear. They have said they will fight and they will."

"So how about this solution…" Astrid cocked her head and twitched her eyes. "Pass the crown to me. I am the eldest and more than capable. I know you know that, Father, in your heart."

Haakon studied his sister's flashing eyes and the determined set of her jaw. She was one of a kind, and *ja*, likely more than capable. But what she didn't realize was she would need a man one day, one she didn't insist on terrifying with her quick temper and knife-sharp wit. Without a man, she wouldn't have the means to have children to continue their line.

"You refused Tyr's marriage proposal, when we were at Uppsala," Haakon said.

"What? *Ja*, of course." She huffed. "He was full of mead and horny. It was not a serious offer."

"It is the third time he has suggested it. Sounds serious to me," the king added.

"We should get on with this day." Astrid huffed.

"No, I want to know why you keep refusing him," Urd said. "Tell me."

Astrid's features tightened, the way they did when her blood was heating and her temper rising. She bit on her bottom lip as though holding in sharp words.

"He is a fine man," Haakon pointed out. "A strong warrior and he has a trade that would support you while you carry sons. His boats are of the finest quality and sought out for miles around."

"And he seeks to please me with gifts and entertain me with walks into the forest. How can I tolerate that?" She blew up her cheeks as though sickened at the thought.

"It sounds perfectly tolerable." Urd nodded slowly. "It was how I wooed your mother."

"I'm surprised she fell for it." Astrid folded her arms. "Such whimsical activities."

"Lucky for you that she did." Urd shrugged.

Astrid frowned. "Tyr agrees with me. He's too agreeable."

"'Too agreeable'?"

"*Ja.*" She held out her hands. "He agrees with everything I say. It is as though he has nothing to say himself."

"Or he is scared to upset you," Haakon said.

"Exactly." She waggled her finger at him. "And who wants to be married to someone who is scared of them?"

Haakon chuckled. "Your problem, Astrid, is that you *are* scary. It is going to take quite a man to stand up to you once he has given you his heart. He will need to be brave to risk having his soul crushed, watch his reason for breathing walk away when he upsets you by not agreeing."

"I doubt there is any such man in these lands," Urd said.

"You may well be right." She folded her arms.

The crowd around them began to chant, parting as Ravn and his wife, Siggy, in her amber-colored cloak made their way from the Great Hall to the makeshift fighting ring.

"May the gods be with you," Astrid said to Haakon. "And more with you than Ravn."

"The day's end is already planned, sister. Now it must be acted out." Haakon's belly tensed and he flexed his limbs. It was time to fight for what was rightfully his.

He glanced at Siggy. She had her hands knotted beneath her chin and was wide-eyed and pale. At her side was her mother, holding Ravn and Siggy's infant son, Thormod. Had the gods planned on her being widowed today? Her son fatherless? Haakon hoped not, but that would mean his own death, so he didn't hope too much.

He didn't want to die. Not yet. He had so much to still see and achieve.

Clutching his shield and with his freshly-sharpened dagger at the ready, Haakon stepped into the ring and up to Ravn.

Like him, Ravn was bare-chested and bare-footed. They stared at each other unblinking.

Orm appeared before them, almost hopping on the spot with excitement. His cloak was a black wolf fur, and the head of the wolf was still in place, pulled up as a glassy-eyed hood. "The brothers are here, and ready. And they're both hungry for victory." He *whooped* and the crowd cheered again. "Kingdom of Drangar!" Orm boomed as he bounced around the fighting circle. "Are you ready for the spectacle of the century? The battle that will go down in history? History not just on Earth, but in the halls of the gods. The fight to the death of the sons of the great King Urd Rhalson of Drangar."

The crowd's excited yells made Haakon's ears ring, but he focused on the task at hand and forced everything else to fade away.

"Today, we will witness the birth and death of a king. One will be victorious in this life; the other will be victorious in feasting with the gods on this day in Valhalla." Orm spun to Ravn. "Will it be Ravn, a mighty warrior, fine horseman, and sharp of mind?" Orm tapped his head and cackled. "Or will it be Haakon?"

He stomped over to Haakon. "Haakon, my brave brother." Orm slapped him on the shoulder.

Haakon snarled.

"The finest seafarer I have ever known," Orm went on, "master hunter and slayer of none other than Dann Erikson, the berserker of the Eastlands."

The crowd cheered wildly, stomping their feet and clapping.

"Both would make an excellent king," Orm shouted. "And it is a decision no mere mortal can make, not even their father, so let us leave it to the fate the gods mapped before the moon and stars were created." He snatched up a shield and withdrew his axe then used the handle to bang the shield wildly. "Let the fight begin. May the best man win!"

Ravn roared and rushed forward, dagger at the ready.

Haakon sidestepped, puffing up grit and stones as he moved. Despite the cold day, he was hot, the blood in his veins boiling with a sudden determination to take his brother's life.

Ravn lunged for Haakon again, but Haakon blocked him with his shield—a thick thud of metal on wood that rattled his teeth together.

He grabbed an opportunity and aimed a swipe at Ravn, catching him on the upper arm. Instantly, blood appeared, but Ravn didn't appear to notice and aimed again at Haakon.

Haakon slipped to the right. He was nimble despite his size and always used that to his advantage.

Ravn swung around, following him. Also fast and light on his feet and annoyingly knowing Haakon's moves.

Haakon spun and took aim, hitting Ravn's shield this time. Ravn backed up, adjusting his hold on his shield.

The crowd yelled and heckled, clearly enjoying the excitement.

"Get the fuck over here!" Haakon bellowed.

"Be careful what you ask for." Ravn snarled and stormed at Haakon, dagger at the ready, shield protecting his torso.

At the last moment, Ravn aimed high and Haakon had to drop to his knees, shield above him. He then rolled to the right, turning over in the dirt before jumping up again. His body was alive with the need for victory.

Ravn grunted in frustration, slamming his fist on his shield, and attacked again.

Haakon stormed forward to meet him, features twisted with fury and determination.

They came together in a great crash. Charging bulls, battling walruses. A tangle of bitter rivalry that shook Haakon's bones.

Then suddenly, a mighty chest blow knocked the wind from his lungs and he fell to the floor. His dagger landed several feet away and his chest refused to expand. He clutched his throat, trying to inhale a ribbon of air. None came. He fell backward.

To his right, Astrid shouted, "No, please, no."

Ravn dropped to the ground with his knees folded on either side of Haakon's upper body. He raised his bloody dagger high and let out a feral roar.

This was it. The gods had spoken. And they'd stolen his ability to breathe moments before Ravn's dagger plunged to be doubly sure of his death.

"Stop! Stop this now!" Suddenly, his father hurled his empty horn of mead into the ring. It rolled to a halt beside Ravn's bent knee. "I order this to stop."

The crowd went silent.

Ravn was staring down at Haakon. The dagger was poised, ready for its deadly plunge.

Haakon's vision blurred, his head felt light and dizzy. This was the moment of his death. How could it not be?

"I command this to stop," Urd said, rushing forward. "I will not lose a son today."

"Father." Orm bounced around him. "It is a fight to the death. That was the agreement and—"

A trickle of air made it into Haakon's lungs. He gasped, trying for more.

"Be quiet, boy!" Urd shook his fist at Orm. "And get out of my sight."

Orm ran in a fast circle, his cloak billowing and his wolf's hood falling down to reveal a freshly shaved hairstyle that left only a long plait falling from the crown of his head.

Urd ignored him and wrapped his hand firmly around Ravn's aloft hands to hold them steady. "This ends now, son. You are king."

"I am king?" Ravn repeated, still staring at Haakon. His arms shook with tension.

"*Ja*, you have won the crown. There is no need to spill your brother's blood."

Haakon managed a proper breath and his vision cleared. Had he heard right? His father had given the crown to Ravn before Haakon's mortal life was over?

It seemed Urd had. Anger instantly replaced the reassignment to death. He glared at Ravn.

"Haakon will always be my enemy if I do not kill him today." Ravn spoke through gritted teeth.

"He is your brother," Urd said. "Now that this matter is settled, he can return to being your brother."

The crowd seemed to be collectively holding their breath. A raven cawed. A wave broke against the shoreline.

"Son, give me the dagger," Urd said.

Ravn raised the dagger, his grip loosening.

Urd took it and straightened with the sticky weapon hanging at his side.

Ravn stood. He spat on the ground then swiped at his bloody, wounded arm.

Haakon pushed to sitting. "I will never accept this." Fury gripped him like a tight fist. "You should have killed me."

Astrid was suddenly squatted at his side. "Brother." She rested her palm on his hot, grimy back. "Are you well?"

"How can I be when I have been cheated? I should be preparing to feast with the gods."

"No, that was not your destiny. Not today. Believe in their wisdom."

How could he? How could he go on? Drangar couldn't be home now. Not for him. It wasn't big enough.

"Good people of Drangar, you have your new king!" Urd clasped Ravn's hand and held it high. "King Ravn, a fine warrior and a fine and fair leader." He swung his attention around to his people. "Show your respects to my son, your new king."

"I am your king!" Ravn pounded his chest with his free hand. "I am victorious. I am your king."

Haakon thought he might vomit.

There were smiles and cheers. It was clear the people were happy with their new young king, who would lead and protect them.

"What the fuck?" Haakon pushed away from Astrid and got to his knees. Slowly, he unfolded and stood. This situation was not acceptable and he had to do something about it. "*He* is not king. We haven't fought to the death." He spotted his dagger and rushed for it.

Quick as a kingfisher's flash, Astrid grabbed it. She held it behind her back and stepped away, her gaze flicking to her father.

"There will be no more fighting on this day," Urd said with his focus on Haakon. "I have no intention of lighting a pyre boat at dusk.

"It was a deal!" Haakon said, slamming a fist against his palm. "There is only room for one of us here."

"Exactly!" Ravn pointed at him. "And that is me. This is *my* kingdom. I will reign over Drangar and all the provinces." He tilted his chin. "You must get used to it, brother."

"I cannot, and I cannot stay here." Haakon swiped the back of his hand over his mouth, wiping away spit and blood. "I cannot breathe the same air as you, Ravn."

"That is preferable to you dying, son," Urd said. "If you leave, I will know you still have life in your veins."

"If I leave, Father, I will never return." Haakon gestured out to sea. "You will never see me again in this, our mortal life."

"But I will know you are out there." Urd gestured out to sea. "Somewhere. 'Haps even happy."

"*Happy*! Huh, after I have had the crown stolen from me." He'd never be happy again. He'd never smile again—he knew that much for certain.

"I won fair and square. I am the stronger warrior." Ravn held up his arms, fists clenched, and turned a circle, as though showing the crowd his bulging muscles.

A cheer went up. Siggy was smiling broadly.

Haakon scowled and his attention went to Urd's new longboat, built by Tyr and stocked ready for the first expedition of the spring. An idea jumped into his head. An excellent idea. "I will leave now," he said, grabbing his tunic and cloak from Joseph. "This very day." He stooped and snatched up his boots, suddenly bursting with the brilliance of this new plan.

"The weather is not suitable." Urd frowned. "And there is so little light each day."

"You said it yourself, Father: I am an excellent seafarer, and that"—he pointed at the harbor—"has no more waves than a bathing barrel. Torches will easily lead the way."

Urd's lips tightened, but he gave no more argument. And Haakon knew why. The sun was going to set and both the king's sons would be alive and he wouldn't do any more to jeopardize that.

Ravn laughed. "It's all very well the harbor water being flat, but out of the fjord, past the mountains, and into open sea, the waves can be as tall as Eagle Cliff and as mean as a hungry bear. You will not last a day and night out there. But you are a fool, always have been, so I am sure you will go, brother."

Haakon pulled on his tunic then wrapped his cloak around himself.

In an instant, he'd shoved his feet into his boots and stowed his dagger on his belt. He faced the crowd, his back to Ravn. "It is the desire of the gods that I go find a fate of my own and not one at the hands of my brother, your new king." He grimaced; the words tasted bitter and uttering them had made their flavor worse. "I bid you all farewell, and you, Father, I wish you peace here with Ravn and his family."

Urd didn't speak.

"You have been banished," Ravn shouted with a pointed finger. "Do not tell the story that you left of your own accord."

"That is exactly what I am doing. This is my choice, my decision." Haakon rushed toward Ravn, his anger re-stoked. "And I would urge you not to tell the story any other way unless you want me to stay and know that you will never sleep easy. If I stay here, under your rule, you will always wonder if tonight is the night your twin slits your throat and takes the crown."

Ravn growled. "I should have slit yours when I had the chance."

"Ravn." Siggy was behind him, tugging his arm, the breeze catching her long, blonde hair. "Please, it is for the best if Haakon leaves. It does not matter who decided it."

Ravn calmed at her touch. He wrapped his arm around her waist and pulled her close. "How does it feel to be the new queen?" He set a hard kiss on her lips.

Haakon snapped his hood over his head and spun around. He marched toward the crowd. They separated, a wave of movement. A hum of conversation rose quickly and a drum beat filled the air.

He stomped onto the pier, his cape flowing behind him and with the familiar thrill an upcoming sea voyage always gave him.

When he'd reached the boat, he jumped nimbly onto it and went to the bow. With one arm wrapped around the serpent's neck, he leaned forward, over the water. "Who will accompany me?" he bellowed.

Silence.

"I know you want to. Come aboard, join me." He fist-pumped the air.

A spread of faces: women, men, children. No raised hands. No excited cries. No rush up the pier toward him.

A claw of doubt scratched at Haakon's confidence. "I know there are bold men amongst you. Men who wish to live a life free of King Ravn's taxes, bad fortune, and certain famine?" He pursed his lips and stared at the crowd. "Do not fail me. Do not fail the gods. They have spoken this day and a new life awaits those who are brave enough to take it."

Chapter Five

SILENCE FELL SUDDENLY—A cold expansion of nothing that spread around the crowd. It spread over the frozen earth and coated the buildings.

Urd hoped someone would volunteer to go with Haakon. It would be certain death for his son to sail alone. There would have been no point saving him from Ravn's dagger.

Then suddenly, a deep voice punctured the quiet. "I will! I will go with him."

Gunnar elbowed from the crowd. A seven-foot giant, he was an experienced sailor and fine warrior. He'd lost his wife and children to the sweating disease the previous winter.

"Excellent!" Haakon pointed at him. "My good friend Gunnar can see a better future with me. Who else will join us?"

"I will. I'm with you."

Urd spotted Egil throwing down the hood of his cape and scooping up a shield and sword.

"It will be an honor to sail with you, Haakon." Egil marched onto the pier, his footfalls heavy thuds.

"The honor is mine." Haakon beamed at him and adjusted his arm ring, which had slipped in the fight.

"Count me in."

"And I."

Two more strong young Vikings stepped forward. They were both skilled hunters and warriors.

Urd glanced at Ravn. His eyebrows were drawn together and his lips flattened. Siggy rested a soothing hand on his upper arm.

"We have a crew," Haakon bellowed. "And so bring in the ropes, we have everything we need. We will hit the seas this very day and start our new life."

"Father," Astrid said, clasping Urd's hand. "Are you really going to let him leave?"

"*Ja*, it is for the best." Urd nodded sadly.

She glanced at Ravn. "It is not the best for me."

"What do you mean?"

"Ravn and I have never…we do not think the same. I fear that if I stay, he will be cruel to me."

"I do not believe that. He is stern, single-minded, but not cruel."

She swallowed and tilted her chin. "When you are feasting with the gods, he will force me to marry and then, when I am a wife and mother, he will refuse me battle when that is what I am trained for. It is what I live for. I am a shield-maiden to my core. It is in every drop of my blood."

Urd suddenly realized what his daughter was saying. "No, don't go." His heart squeezed. "I beg you, Astrid."

"I have to." Her eyes quickly filled with moisture. A tear escaped the right one and ran swiftly down her cheek. She swiped irritably at it. "I cannot stay here. Not without Mother, not without you."

"But I am still here," Urd said. "I am not dead and in the company of the gods just yet."

"Which makes it near impossible to leave."

"*Near* impossible."

She threw her arms around him, embracing him tightly. "I'm sorry, Father. I am so sorry. I'm sorry."

He clung to her, breathing in her sweet, lavender scent, and closed his eyes. What did the future hold for his wild daughter? He didn't know, but what he did know was he wouldn't be around to see it…he wouldn't be around to help her.

"Haakon will look out for you. I know he will," he said with a croak of emotion in his voice. If he'd crowned Haakon, his beloved, misunderstood daughter would be staying. But it was too late to change the fates now. "I agree with your decision."

"You do?" She pulled back, her cheeks wet and blotched now.

"*Ja*, he loves you, as do I."

"Thank you for understanding."

"Understanding doesn't mean I want you to leave." He touched her cheek. "You are a knotted soul, Astrid, with all the twisted kinks of both myself and your mother. I wish you well, I wish your future husband well, and your unborn children." He paused. "And I will give offerings to the gods to look down on you from their feasting table."

"Thank you. Thank you." She kissed each of his cheeks then sniffed loudly.

"I will see you in another realm, my beautiful daughter, and we will feast and dance and be merry."

"We will, Father." With a flick of her cloak, she strode from him.

His arms ached instantly. Astrid was the only daughter he'd been blessed with, and although her antics as a child had caused his hair to gray faster than it should have, and her stubbornness as an adult had given him stomach pains at times, he'd miss her desperately.

"Goodbye, brother Ravn." She waved her hand at the new king.

"And where are you going?" he snapped.

"With Haakon!" She threw her head back and laughed then broke into a run, holding the handle of her dagger with one hand and shield with the other. "Wait! Wait for me, brother."

"Astrid! Come back here!" Ravn shouted. "I order you, as your king, do not leave Drangar!"

"You can't fucking stop me!" She carried on running.

"Astrid!" Ravn clenched his fists and broke away from his wife. "Get back here—now." His brow was marked by three deep frown lines. "I demand it."

Astrid ignored him and leaped onto the boat.

A gruff cheer went up from the men inside. She was well respected as a hard worker and they knew the more hands on deck, the better off they'd be.

"And so she escapes." Orm spun a circle in front of Urd's face. "The flame-haired beauty who has you wrapped around her finger, Father." He laughed. "So much so that you do not order her back even when the new king commands it. You allow her to disobey the first order he has given."

"It is right that she goes," Urd said, flicking his hand and wishing he could flick Orm away.

"Ah, and is it right that Haakon go too?" Orm stood still and raised his eyebrows.

"*Ja*, I believe it is preferable to his death on this day."

"So you are happy to see your children leave this town, this land? This cold, barren, crop-less land, a place that holds a future of famine and sickness and war."

"Orm, watch what you say. Odin sees everything, remember. He will not like you making your own predictions."

Orm pressed his finger to his lips. "Watch what I say…I can do that, but I will say one last thing before I start watching." He flung back his head, eyes closed, and shouted at the sky. "Goodbye, Drangar! I bid you farewell. And, Father, I bid you farewell too, which is what you've always wanted—to see me gone. Out of sight. You said it yourself. Out of sight. Well, now you can celebrate because not one, not two, but three of your children are leaving. Your favorite number—you are indeed blessed. Three of us are leaving you."

"Orm! Do not…"

But Urd was speaking to Orm's back because Orm had taken off, following in the footsteps of his brother and sister. He sprinted through the crowd with a wild *whoop* and then raced along the pier, the wolf head of his cape bobbing on his back.

The longboat, now unmoored, was creeping away from its dock, a black void spreading beneath it.

"Wait for me!" Orm yelled, excitement ripping through his voice. "Brother dearest, sister, oh, sweet one, wait for me! Wait. For. Me."

He sped up, then hurtled himself into the air, arms and legs flailing.

The crowd watched enraptured. Eyes wide.

Would he make it?

And then he landed on the boat with a loud *whump* and a call of glee. He punched the air and clung to a rope. "Goodbye, Father. Goodbye, Ravn. I miss you already!" He laughed excitedly. "Whoops! No, I don't."

And just like that, Urd had said goodbye to not one, but three children. All bound for the high seas and new adventures. Was he sad? *Ja*, of course he was. Astrid held a special place in his heart, and he knew he was one of the few people she truly loved. Haakon, he was glad he was alive, and Orm, well, life would be easier without his crazy youngest child around.

So he hoped only good things for them, a life free of the gods' anger and full of love and dreams.

It was all he could do now. Hope.

HAAKON DUCKED TO avoid being lashed once more by a wild wave. It was as though the sea were boiling beneath them. Bubbling, rolling, slapping up against itself, and whipping the wooden hull of the boat.

His crew was struggling to maintain control. Heck, staying upright and holding their oars was hard enough.

Above them, gulls circled, hoping for food, calling to one another. But they wouldn't get anything. The stocks aboard the new longboat had not been as plentiful as Haakon had hoped and he'd berated himself countless times during the last weeks for not checking before spontaneously leaping on deck and setting sail.

"We need to find land," Astrid called as she heaved back on an oar. She'd battled the ocean as well as any man. Strong and healthy, she had steely determination.

"For the love of Freya, there must be land," Orm yelled over a clap of thunder. "There are gulls." He also dragged on an oar. "They nest somewhere."

"They can fly many miles." Haakon wiped the sea salt from his eyes and stared into the distance. The watery horizon had blurred into the raven-black sky. The clouds were as menacing as Thor's hammer and likely as heavy too.

But that was north and they were traveling west, hoping to strike a bay or harbor in Lothlend. He'd been to this green, hilly land with Ravn a few years ago. They'd come across a small settlement ripe for the picking. The people's treasures were conveniently housed in one place, a large structure called a "church" with windows full of colored glass. And the people had cowered, cried, pleaded for their lives as Haakon and Ravn, along with their men, had piled up a cart and taken everything shiny and bejeweled they could find.

Upon their return, Urd had been so pleased with the stash, he'd thrown a huge banquet for everyone in Drangar and sacrificed three goats to Odin.

The boat lurched to the right then tilted to the left. Another wave broke against them, sending spray over their last barrel of drinking water.

They were getting desperate. Haakon was beginning to wonder if this was in fact the worst situation he'd ever found himself in out at sea. And if it was, he could kick himself for the fact Astrid was on the boat.

If anything happened to her, he'd never forgive himself.

"Maybe it has started. Ragnarök is here!" Gunnar shouted through a mouthful of sea spray. "And this isn't just the end of us, but the end of the world and all the mighty gods."

"If it is, we will fight like the warriors we are," Orm yelled, holding his face to the black sky. He let out a blood-curdling shriek.

A forked bolt of lightning streaked overhead. It was followed by the raging, thunderous drumming of Thor, and then more lightning flashed in big, blinding sheets.

Haakon stared west, clinging to two ropes as the boat went nearly up on its aft as it struck a wave head on.

There. What was that?

His heart rate picked up. A nugget of hope dared to reveal itself. Had he seen the tiny flicker of flames? If so, there must be land.

He waited for the next curtain of brilliant bright light to fill the sky. And when it did, he saw it.

A curved beach lined with a cliff and a forest.

"Over there," he yelled, pointing and almost falling overboard because he'd let go of his hold and the boat was pitching downward. "Land. Land. This is an omen that we will survive. The gods are indeed with us."

"Land? Where?" Orm said, standing but quickly being knocked back to his seat. He resumed rowing.

"*Ja*. Land, to the west. Turn, turn that way." Haakon dropped down and grabbed an oar. He threw his strength into turning the trajectory of the boat. His strong crew helped and a full-on battle with the monstrous waves began.

He was wet through, but sweat still soaked his armpits and the gutter of his spine. He huffed and puffed, a rush of energy in his veins pushing him on. "Keep going. Keep going. We will not be defeated by Njord. His wily ways with wind and sea will not take our souls this day."

"Njord, be appeased," Orm shouted from beneath his wolf hood.

"And we will honor you with many sacrifices." He was breathless. "And send you many virgins…if you bless us with mercy."

"Pull! Pull!" Haakon yelled, getting the rowers in synchrony. "Keep going."

Astrid was working hard, her hair plastered to her face and her eyes alive with the battle. She grunted and pulled, strong and fearlessly.

Soon, he would have her on dry land. It was a promise he made to himself.

A wave curled overhead, a sea serpent of froth and spray and icy arrowheads. It hit Haakon full-on in the face, but he spat the water from his mouth and didn't pause heaving on his oar.

Gunner sat to his right. He'd removed his wet fur cloak and tunic and his cold flesh sparkled, his muscles bunching and flexing beneath his skin. He grunted with each lunge on his oar, his dark eyes narrowed and his teeth gritted.

"We're not far now," Haakon shouted. "We will make this landfall."

"To the land!" Astrid yelled.

A chorus of shouts and *whoops*. The sail clapped, the hull creaked, and the ropes strained.

A sudden, deafening bang. The boat rolled to the right. Egil dropped his oar and was sent flying backward, legs in the air.

Astrid screamed as her oar was ripped from her hand and taken overboard.

"What the fuck?" Orm yelled.

"We've hit rock," Haakon said, watching in horror as the wooden planks beneath his feet splintered upward and the sea rushed in to circle his ankles. "We're being torn apart."

"Land is just there," Orm yelled. "We'll have to swim for it."

"In this ugly water?" Gunnar said, gripping the side of the boat and pushing up from the water that had engulfed his seat. "We will die."

"We will die here. We have no choice," Astrid said, also standing. "Pray the gods are with you and that you live to see the sun again."

A huge wave cascaded over her, frothing, sizzling, thumping, and when it receded Astrid was no longer on the boat.

"Sister!" Orm cried, standing.

"Abandon. Swim. That way!" Haakon stood up on the side of the boat, clutching a rope. He spotted the land, clearer now—a forest-lined sandy bay—then swept his scrutiny over the black, foreboding water, searching desperately for Astrid.

She was nowhere to be seen. "Astrid! Astrid!" His stomach lurched. His heart thudded. "Where are you?"

There was nothing else for it. He hurled himself into the air. A punch to his side as he was hit by a wave, then nothingness turned to freezing water, the chill of it like a thousand daggers driving into his flesh.

The bellowing wind was replaced by the crash of water in his ears. He was tossed this way and that but saw dusky daylight and kicked, struggling against the weight of his cape and boots.

Bursting upward, he gasped for air and was hit in the face with sharp hailstones—adding to his torment. And right in front of him, the hull of the stricken boat loomed, black, huge, and hurtling toward him at speed.

A searing pain over his temple.

Then…blackness.

Chapter Six

THE SKY ABOVE Kenna had turned to the color of wet peat. The air had an ethereal glow, as though being lit by amber; it gave the snowy ground a strange, creamy hue. As she turned to Hamish, a huge dot of rain landed on the tip of her nose. "We are in for a rainstorm. It will melt some of this snow, but it will soak us through."

"You are right, sister." He pulled up the tasseled hood of his black cloak. "And it is coming soon."

"We won't make it back to the village before it pours," Bryce said. "We should find shelter nearby."

"Aye, I agree." Kenna settled the bag of hazelnuts she'd been foraging securely in her linen bag and glanced at the ocean. It was wild, as though excited at the thought of the storm dumping more water into its mass. Waves lurched upward, their white tips colliding and curling. It was no longer possible to see the horizon, the sheets of rain in the distance having obscured it.

"To the shore," Hamish said. "We'll go into a cave. It can't last long."

"Good idea." Kenna set off at a sprint, her brother and Bryce close behind. "Come on! You're so slow!"

They weren't slow at all. The two men were hot on her tail as the path turned sodden. She wound around a copse of firs and then down a slope, almost slipping on the slushy surface. A deer and fawn ran in front of her, wide-eyed and their coats wet and shiny. They were gone as quickly as they'd appeared.

A huge bellow of thunder drummed overhead, seeming to vibrate right through to her bones as she raced along, legs pounding. It was accompanied by a blaze of lightning so bright, it blinded her for several seconds.

But she didn't stop running. She'd seen a fork hit a tree a few years ago. Watched the ancient trunk being ripped in two, sliced as though it were butter. She didn't fancy that happening to her.

"Go left," Bryce called from behind her. "Down onto the sand."

She was already heading that way, intent on reaching the caves at the end of the forest track. They were her safety.

Her feet sunk into wet sand and she dashed at the rain dripping down her face. She could taste it, pure and cool. Her cloak was sopping, but she hoped her clothes beneath would be dry so she didn't catch a chill as they waited for the storm to pass.

Hamish overtook her then was swallowed by darkness as he ran into the first cave they reached.

Kenna followed him, jumping a small rivulet that was running down the hill. She reached the front of the cave entrance and then parted ivy tendrils to get inside.

"Thank God for these caves," Bryce said, coming to a skidding halt as he too entered the cave.

"It's not the first time they've saved us in a storm," Kenna said. "Remember that time we got caught out with the first fall of snow?"

Hamish chuckled and shrugged out of his wet cloak, laying it on a rock. "Aye, and didn't we promise to always have a stash of firewood on hand in these caves?"

"Is there wood in this one?" Bryce asked hopefully as she moved to the back of the cave where a low, smooth rock lay flat.

"I bloody hope so," Kenna said, peering into the darkness.

"Aye, here." Hamish held up a bundle of kindling. "There're a few logs too."

"Get it started," Kenna said, also taking off her wet cloak. "We can stay warm and dry out."

Hamish dropped to his knees and quickly arranged the kindling.

Bryce added dried weed and then flicked sparks from a flint at it.

Within minutes, the first flames were licking upward, their delicate heat giving the promise of more to come and sending shadows into the cave.

"This is good." Kenna held her hands to the warmth. "We can wait it out here."

"Hopefully, it will pass quickly. The wind is so strong, it will push the clouds away."

"I hope so." She pulled a handful of hazelnuts from her bag and set about eating them.

"I need to pee," Hamish said, slipping out of the front of the cave to the overhang.

Bryce sat on a piece of driftwood near the fire and rubbed his hands together.

Kenna sat opposite, on a cold, round rock.

With a gush of energy, the rain intensified, the noise suddenly deafening. The rain had turned to hail; big, white balls of ice were now battering the land. She watched it gathering in drifts around the rocks lining the beach. Several bounced into the cave, landing near her boots.

"Look!" Hamish was suddenly at her side pointing out to sea. "Do you see that?"

There was a note of alarm in his voice and quickly, Kenna swung her attention to the sea. The waves were still wild, the sky still blackened by rushing rain clouds.

A sheet of lightning made the watery view glow white.

"Oh, fuck!" She stood, the nuts falling from her hand. "It's a longboat."

"Norsemen!" Bryce was on his feet now, and even through the dim light, she could see he'd paled.

"They're not faring well." Hamish tapped the dagger on his belt as though checking it was there. "As nobody would in this bay and on this hellish sea."

"They've been spotted a few times, farther out, but sailed right on past us," Bryce said. "Not even pausing."

"I'm not sure they could pass us by today, even if that was their intention." Kenna watched the curved bow of the boat reach for the sky as the aft dipped into the waves. The sail snapped this way and that, seeming to keep changing its mind as to the direction of the wind.

"Is there anyone on it?" Bryce asked.

"Aye." Hamish pointed again. "I can see. There. Someone standing at the helm."

Kenna clasped her hand over her mouth. She could see the ogre too, and he was pointing her way.

"They will be drowned and if not drowned, smashed to pieces on the rocks," Hamish said. "God will protect us from them. He'll use the sea to rid these parasites from our lands."

"What if God shows *them* mercy?" Kenna asked. "As we ask him to show us mercy and forgiveness."

"What they have done, if the stories are true, is not something even our benevolent Lord could forgive."

"Aye, they are brutes, evil brutes. They take what is not theirs, they murder and maim." Bryce spat on the floor. "I hope they all drown like the rats they are."

"I think you might get your wish, Bryce. Can you see that?" Hamish peered forward through the waterfall of hail. "It looks like they have struck rock."

"Impossible not to in this bay." Kenna knew it well. The callous rocks lurked beneath the surface, only visible at the lowest of tides. They were a good defense.

Usually.

"They are breaking apart. The boat doesn't stand a chance," Bryce said excitedly.

Sure enough, she could see it separating, as though a giant had snapped it in half. The mast lurched left and right and then fell, the sail dipping into the water. And while it did that, the crew of beastly brutes hurtled themselves into the mercy of the sea.

They watched in silence. The hail eased and turned once more to rain, and after a minute, a slice of bright-blue sky appeared in the east.

But the waves didn't appease. They were feral, wild animals gnashing and snarling. No one would survive their violent wrath. If a boat couldn't survive, what hope did bones, flesh, and blood have?

Kenna sat again, though she didn't stop staring at the sea, wondering about the souls drowning. What would it feel like? Would it be a panic to breathe or would it be peaceful once fate had been accepted? And would God take these bad souls to heaven or would they be sent straight to burn in hell for all eternity?

Bryce stooped and added a log to the fire. Several sparks burst upward.

"They must be dead," Hamish said, also sitting. "Battered onto the rocks, skulls smashed, I should think."

"Let's pray for that," Bryce said.

Kenna said nothing. She couldn't quite bring herself to pray for smashed skulls, even those of her enemies. It really didn't seem very Christian.

"The rain is stopping," Bryce said a few minutes later.

Kenna looked at the sky; the bright patch was growing. It was true, the storm was blowing itself away and what had felt like night was turning back to a winter's day.

She dug into her pocket and pulled out a fresh handful of nuts, popped a few into her mouth, and chewed.

"We should get back to the village," Hamish said, kicking sand onto the fire. "Tell Father what we have seen."

"He will rejoice in the deaths of Norsemen." Bryce chuckled and stood. He shook out his cloak. "And I thank God for saving us from their brutality."

Kenna stood. She swung her cloak over her shoulders. "I will be glad to get back within the village walls. Any day we see those monsters is not a good day."

She stepped from the cave, her feet crunching on a drift of hailstones. The boat was in bits now; several of its long planks of wood were being tossed on the waves. There was no sign of the devilish crew.

"Come on, let's go." Bryce strode past her, making for the track that led up the sandy bank.

Hamish followed, his strides purposeful.

Kenna stood for a moment, watching the waves.

And then she saw it. A body.

Dark and big, it was being pushed toward the land with each curl of the waves.

"Look!" She stepped forward, pointing. "Can you see that?"

No reply.

She swung around, but Bryce and Hamish had already been swallowed by the forest.

Curiosity gnawed at her—an inquisitiveness so intense, she couldn't ignore it. She stepped onto the wet sand with her heart racing and her breaths puffing out in front of her face.

She pulled up her hood and rushed toward the sea. With each step, she could see the body getting closer. It had hit land now and was being pushed and pulled with each ebb and flow of the waves.

A finger of sunlight poked through the clouds, hitting the water he lay in.

And it was a *he*, a man, she was sure. No woman would be that big.

With splashing footsteps, she drew closer. He was on his stomach.

His sodden tunic clinging to his muscular torso, his sea-soaked fur cape scrunched to one side. His dark hair was long and his boots worn but fine quality.

She didn't really know what came over her—perhaps it was instinct, or an innate nosiness, or maybe it was her Christian upbringing—but she stooped, grabbed the material at his shoulders, and heaved him up the shoreline.

Grunting, she dragged him free from the waves. He was lifeless and as heavy as a rock. She stumbled then fell to her ass, only to quickly jump up and drag him a little further.

When the waves were just tickling his feet, she dropped to her knees at his side. Her brother and Bryce would berate themselves for running off so quickly, because now it was she, Kenna, who was going to be the first in the village to get an up-close look at a Viking.

Summoning strength, she shoved at him, once, twice, trying to push him over to his back. It took a few hard heaves—he wasn't light and with the added weight of his wet clothes, it took all of her strength. But then he landed on his back, his arms falling to his sides and his head lolling.

She gasped. He was indeed a monster. His neck and throat were a mass of ink, and his muscles bulged. Sand clung to his strong jawline and his big, straight nose. His eyebrows were also dusted with wet sand, as was his forehead. Around his neck on a piece of leather was a boar fang. She knew that was what it was—she'd recognize one of those anywhere.

Her attention slid down his body, his tunic was ripped, showing most of his chest, and a belt around his hips held a dagger with a shiny bone handle. His pants were dark and a piece of glossy seaweed clung to the material at his groin.

She hovered her shaking hand over his chest. He was dead, she was sure of it. He'd drowned in the storm. But even so, she wanted to check, so she gently rested her palm on his chest. His flesh was solid, chilled but somehow warmish too.

And then she felt it. *Thud, thud, thud.* The unmistakable beating of his heart.

He wasn't dead. He was alive.

She gasped and withdrew her hand. Looked back up at his face.

His eyes were wide open. Piercing blue, they stared at her, unblinking.

With a squeal, she fell backward, onto her behind, then quickly scrambled to her feet, kicking up sand.

Without a backward glance, she took off at a run, toward the forest, toward Bryce and Hamish.

As far away from the hideous beach monster as she could get.

Chapter Seven

HAAKON STARED UP at his Valkyrie. He'd had good fortune. She was incredibly beautiful. But then he was a prince—it was no wonder he was being escorted to Valhalla by the most beautiful of all the Great Hall's guides.

Hair the color of chestnuts curled around the hood of her dark, ethereal cloak. Her skin was flawless, and so pale and delicate. Her lips reminded him of a spring rosebud and her eyes, so green, as green as a lush meadow on the warmest of spring days.

The thud of his heart increased when she rested her gentle hand on his cold, aching flesh. He wanted her to touch him all over. Heal him. Rid him of the pain in his head and the agony of cold in his fingers and toes.

Heat flowed from her to him and he waited for his soul to lift from his mortal body. Any second now, he would float upward, with her, and they'd gallop on great, white horses into the next realm. He'd be happy and content, joyful, knowing feasts and virgins awaited.

He'd clang mead mugs and shout *skål* with Orm and Astrid if they were there, his mother too. It would indeed be a great day.

But nothing happened. He lay there, on the hard sand, waiting for her to clasp his hand and take him. Behind her was the brilliant light of the sky, the storm long gone. A distant memory now that he was dead.

She looked up at his face again.

Her eyes widened, panic filled them. She let out a strangled gasp and suddenly was gone.

He blinked, breathed in, but air wasn't flowing properly into his lungs.

As sand flicked against his face, Haakon pushed forward to sitting. It felt like there was a tight band around his chest. Suddenly, instead of traveling to Valhalla, he was gasping for breath and coughing. He spat salt water. It also poured from his nose. His entire body hurt as he managed to drag in ribbons of air and re-inflate his lungs.

His temple throbbed and he tried to think what had done the damage. Then it came back to him. The boat being torn apart, his leap overboard and then the huge fractured hull the waves had thrown at him.

Finally breathing more normally, he groaned and rubbed his head. Where on Earth was he?

He looked around for signs of life. The Valkyrie had gone. Clearly, him being alive had spooked her and she'd made off without him. He hoped when his time did come, it would be her again, that she was the one destined to be his beautiful guide. If that were the case, there was no reason for him to fear death.

A wave reached his feet then fizzed on the sand as it retreated. He clambered to standing and scrutinized the horizon for signs of the battered boat and his crew.

"Astrid!" he bellowed, turning to the hooked point of the beach. "Orm! Where the fuck are you?"

Nothing. He pressed his hands on his thighs, stooped, and coughed some more, spitting out salt and sand.

Then he straightened and looked around properly. He appeared to be on the beach he'd spotted from the boat. The horseshoe shape of the cove was familiar, as was the rise of the pine forest from a small collection of caves.

"Astrid!" he shouted again, looking to his right. Surely, he hadn't been the only one to make it ashore. "Orm!" Fate wouldn't have been so cruel…would it?

And then he spotted it, movement in the distance against the waves.

He broke into a run, pounding along the wet sand and breathing heavily.

"Astrid!" he called again. It was her. He was sure of it. Gunner too—they were staggering together from the curling waves.

"Thanks be to Odin," he said breathlessly. "She's alive."

He raced to her, relief swamping him.

"Brother!" she shouted into the wind when she saw him. "You made it."

He reached her and cupped her face. A streak of blood ran from a mauve bruise beneath her right eye. "Are you well?"

"Nothing a good fire and feed won't cure." She laughed then turned to Gunner. "Did you see Orm out there?"

"No, only you." Gunner pushed his wet hair back from his face. His bare chest glistened with seawater. "We really bloody angered the gods for that to happen."

"Or pleased them and that is why we still walk and talk," Astrid said with a huff as she pulled out her rune stones, checking they were safely in the small, leather pouch she kept on her belt.

"Yet now we are stranded in a strange land and with no boat." Gunner spat into the sea. "And no boat builder."

"That is a truth." Haakon placed his hands on his hips and studied the forest. "We must be in Lothlend, though which part, I do not know." He paused and sighed. "I hope they speak the language of my father's thrall, Joseph—he taught me much of it."

"'May God forgive you of all your sins!'" Astrid twittered in a mocking voice in the language of their slave, Joseph. "'And have mercy on you heathen children.'"

Gunner chuckled. "I know not what you say, but it sounds ridiculous."

"It is," Astrid said with a dismissive wave. "These people only have one god, you know, for everything. Can you imagine how busy he must be day and night? How little feasting he does or how often he has time to bed virgins?"

"Come," Haakon said with a chuckle. "Let us light a fire and dry out before nightfall." He pointed at the caves. "We'll go over there. Maybe Orm and Egil will find us. Maybe the others too. The firelight will guide them."

"I will first search the shore," Gunner said, striding to the right. "And bring anything I find that is useful. Hopefully, I will find my tunic and cape."

Haakon nodded then set off for the caves. Astrid strode alongside him, checking her dagger for signs of damage. "There is little snow here compared to home."

"That is a good thing, is it not?"

"*Ja*, it is. For us and for crops." She looked up. "It is lighter too. At home, the sky would barely see the sun this time of year."

He glanced at her. "These things make this a good place to settle and farm." As they walked, the cogs of his mind worked. He'd left Drangar forever. He did need somewhere to call home. Somewhere with good soil, more temperate weather, bountiful seas. Some winter sunlight would be a bonus too.

Was this place it?

Was this cove and this forest his destiny?

They reached the first cave. It was shallow with a low roof. The next had roots creeping through cracks in the rock and there'd been a collapse. The final cave had the remnants of a fire.

Astrid stooped beside it and settled her hand over the charcoaled log half covered in sand. "This is still warm." She frowned up at him.

"What?" He also stooped and felt it for himself. "You're right."

"Which means..." She waggled her eyebrows. "We're not alone."

"Someone has been here recently. Perhaps recently enough to see us land." He checked for his dagger. Luckily it was still safely tucked into his belt. "And then run off to gather an army to attack us."

Astrid laughed. "These people couldn't gather an army if they tried. Look how easy they are to raid."

"Maybe not, but we are few and there might be many of them."

"They are likely in their churches, polishing their god's treasures. They will not be interested in us."

"I'm not so sure." He reached for a convenient pile of kindling and stacked it over the ash. He'd get it lit so they could dry out and stay warm. "Our people have somewhat of a reputation for theft and mayhem. If I were them and warriors like us had just landed on our shores, even just a few of us, I'd be sharpening my sword and axe."

Astrid was quiet as she sat on a log and held her hands to the unlit fire. "Come on, get this going."

"I lost my flint."

"Here's a piece." She plucked a sharp, shiny rock from the floor. "This land certainly is giving."

"Another good omen." He noticed a small scattering of hazelnuts near to where Astrid had plucked the flint. Someone had been eating around their fire.

"Let us see what else is in store." She shook her bag of rune stones. "Here, you pick."

He took three stones and handed them to her.

Then as Haakon got the flames started, she tossed them onto the floor in front of her. "Oh... Well, that is very interesting."

"What do they say?" Haakon asked.

"I see so many things." She looked up at him with wide eyes. "That for a woman with a cold heart I find hard to believe."

"You do not have a cold heart." He tended the flames and then carefully set a small log to catch.

"Ha, you are kind, dear brother, but I have been told so by many men." She shrugged.

"I believe they were just scared of you. Maybe one day, you will meet your match and he will warm your heart."

She rolled her eyes dismissively. "Whatever... Look, you see how your stones have fallen."

"And?"

"They have all landed facing you."

"What does that mean?"

"It means these stones are speaking to you with a very loud voice."

"And what are they saying so loudly?" He removed his wet cape, sat, and held his hands to the flames.

"This is the symbol of Ingwaz...fertility."

Haakon said nothing, waiting for his sister to go on.

"It means new beginnings, which we've just spoken about, but it's positive, saying that there is new life, or in your case, *your* new life...here."

"It is affirmative, that's true." He pointed. "What's that one?"

"Ah, this is also a good stone to pull. It's Othala, which is traditionally about inheritance—"

"Huh, I have inherited nothing. Ravn has taken everything from us."

She waggled her finger. "But that is in the past. What this stone is telling you is you must let go of that and other outdated ideas and loyalties. This is about learning anew, being bold and brave and independent."

Haakon nodded slowly. "Good, *ja*."

"And this..." Astrid shifted on her seat as though excited. "Is the best one of all."

"Go on." He frowned and watched the glow of the flames dance on her pretty face.

"This is Odin's rune. It means he is looking down on you right now." She paused and glanced out at the shoreline as though seeing Odin himself. "And he is saying anything is possible and anything can happen. What you have done, and what you have become, has made you ready for this. Choose a direction and go for it. But..." She lowered her voice. "You have to commit to it. Stick with your decision."

"Odin's rune." Haakon nodded slowly. "I am indeed honored and I will stick with my decision to settle here, to learn." He pointed at the stone Othala and then Ingwaz. "And make a new life. And, sister, I am glad you are here too."

"As am I. The gods mapped out our fate together and I'm not complaining." She paused. "I wish for Orm to join us...do you think he will?" Her mouth downturned and a frown line etched across her brow.

Haakon rubbed his chin and looked out to sea. "He is a strong swimmer, and determined too. If there was a way for him to survive, he will have."

Suddenly, a small pebble landed near his feet.

"What the fuck?" Haakon looked upward.

Another landed, and another. Sharp, little clicks. Round, little stones.

Astrid jumped up, her dagger at the ready.

Haakon did the same, instantly ready to fight an army if necessary.

The stones kept coming, until they were raining down the way the hail had earlier.

"Show yourself," Astrid said, peering at the top of the cave entrance. "Let us see your face." She'd spoken in the local language.

It was clear, like Haakon, she was expecting angry Lothlenders to attack.

There was a sudden scramble, more stones, mud, grass, and roots too. Then two wet, leather boots came into view, then sodden breeches, a belt buckle, a dagger Haakon recognized, and finally, the base of a sopping-wet torso.

"Orm!" Astrid said, yanking the right leg that was dangling in the cave entrance.

"Argh!" Orm suddenly appeared, falling through the air then landing, luckily, on a pile of weed and sand.

"In the name of all the gods, what are you doing?" Haakon said, shaking his head and laughing with relief that his brother was alive.

"I wanted to surprise you." Orm sat and adjusted his dripping wolf cape. "You know, surprise you that I was alive."

"You did that." Haakon re-sheathed his dagger.

"And nearly got yourself killed in the process." Astrid waggled her dagger at him before putting it away. "I was about to stab you in your cock."

"I am glad you didn't." Orm grinned. "I saw the god Njord, Njord himself, beneath the waves." He shook his head, sending a spray of sand into the air. "I thought today was my day and I had taken my last breath, and then suddenly from the dark depths came this great, wise face. His watery eyes stared into mine and his whalebone crown glinted silver. Across his chest was a great bow and arrow made from fish guts and shells."

"Did he speak?" Astrid asked, sitting and collecting her rune stones, her attention firmly on Orm. "Did he say anything?"

Orm tapped the side of his head. "He didn't need to speak with his mouth. He was talking to my head, straight into it."

"Saying what?" Haakon asked, wishing his Valkyrie had spoken to him. Just one word would have sufficed.

"He told me to reach for the light," Orm said. "To swim, to fight for breath, and then fight for the shore. He told me today wasn't my last day, that I had to follow my destiny and not alter it by drowning right there, beneath the waves." He pointed out to sea. "Those monster waves. The great serpent is lashing them up with his restless, slithering body."

"I am glad you didn't die, brother." Haakon squeezed his shoulder. "Because this is a new start for us. The rune stones have also spoken, and I have a feeling this land will be bountiful in many ways."

"Look," Astrid said, nodding to the right. "There is Gunner coming toward us, and it looks like Egil, Ivar, and Knud are with him."

"The gods have been good to us," Haakon said. "We will show our thanks as soon as we can. We have not lost one soul in a storm that felt like the start of Ragnarök."

"I was expecting to see the great serpent rise from the ocean at any moment." Orm shuddered. "And pierce me with its fangs."

"Jarl Haakon," Gunner called as he held up his hand. In the other, he held what looked like a wet tunic and cloak. "We end the day as a complete crew."

"For which I am thankful." Haakon slapped Egil on the back, then did the same to Ivar and Knud. "I had a good boat but even better men. Thanks be to Odin."

"It was wild out there," Egil said, swiping his sandy palms together. His hair was still dripping. "But here…now…there is even some blue sky over there."

"Soon, it will be dark," Astrid said, adjusting the log on the fire then adding another piece of driftwood.

"*Ja*, we will rest here overnight, dry out, and tomorrow explore this new place," Haakon said.

"We will hope for treasures to steal." Knud laughed and rubbed his hands together over the fire. "And women. I could take two right now." He laughed harder and thrust his hips back and forth. "One straight after the other."

Haakon said nothing. He'd have to choose his words wisely with his men. For he had no intention of raiding and pillaging. This was his new home. This was land he wanted to claim and then settle upon.

It would be more helpful to be friendly with the locals rather than murder them. He wanted to learn about their way of farming, their crops. Maybe even ask them about their one god too.

"Here." Ivar dropped a pile of glossy, green seaweed beside the fire. "Our food for tonight."

Chapter Eight

KENNA RACED TOWARD Tillicoulty. Her chest hurt, she'd run so fast, and her thighs were on fire with the effort.

There was no lookout on the watchtower. Likely, he was busy collecting firewood before it got dark. She rushed into the settlement, looking around at the scattering of people, searching for her father.

"Where is he?" she muttered, coming to a halt beside the well. She placed her hands on her hips and stooped, dragging in breath.

"Kenna, where'd you go?" Bryce asked, suddenly appearing from a small herd of sheep who stood in a covered pen eating hay.

She straightened, closed her eyes for a second, then blew out a breath. She looked at him. "I went down to the beach."

"Why?" He folded his arms and shook his head. "We were worried. I thought you were right behind us."

"I saw one of them."

"You what?" His eyes widened.

"I saw one of the Norsemen. He was washed up on the waves."

"Dead?"

"I thought so...but..."

"'But'?" Bryce swallowed and glanced at the gate as if expecting a raid at any moment.

"But no, he wasn't dead, because when I touched him—"

"Fuck! You touched him! Are you crazy? Do you have a death wish? In God's name, Kenna." He inspected her from head to foot, as though checking for signs of crazy.

"Of course not. He wasn't breathing, but when I touched him he dragged in a breath and sat up coughing."

"You should have stabbed him through the heart. While he was down." He flapped his arms at the gate. "Because it's only a matter of time before he marches through there to plunder our meager possessions and take whatever woman appeals to his warped mind."

Kenna swallowed. Just the thought of the big brute marching into Tillicoulty and picking a woman to bed sent a shiver up her spine. What if he picked her? She'd be no match for his strength despite being a keen shot with an arrow and deft with her dagger.

"You have to tell your father. The *toísech* needs to know about this."

"Why do you think I ran back so fast?" She frowned. "Of course I need to tell him. Where is he?"

"He called a gathering in the Great House the moment Hamish and I returned and told him what we had seen, but now…now your news makes this matter even more important."

"I know. And we need a lookout on the watchtower. This is no time to be complacent."

"I will see to it."

"Good." She flicked her hair over her shoulders, brushed down her skirt, then marched to the Great House, avoiding several deep puddles caused by melting snow. A fire basket was lit outside, sending smoke into the darkening sky—the light was leaking from the horizon and being replaced with bruised purples. Soon, it would be night.

"Father," she said, bursting in then stopping when she saw the fifteen village elders sitting with her father all in stony silence.

"Kenna." He frowned at her. "We are having a council meeting."

"I can see that." She cleared her throat and set back her shoulders. "But there is something I must tell you."

"We are very busy." He folded his arms and nodded at the doorway she'd just burst through. "We can speak at home."

"No." She stepped into the rough circle in which they all sat. "This cannot wait."

"Kenna, I—"

"They're here." She flicked her hand in the direction of the coast. "They have landed. Or at least one of them has." She was still panting. "Vikings. Here."

Her father's lips flattened and his eyebrows pulled low. "Hamish reported that the crew of the Viking boat you saw had perished."

"They did." Hamish folded his arms and rocked back on his heels. He was standing beside the fire holding a cup of ale.

"That is what we thought. The storm was fierce, the waves murderous. But it seems the ocean was unsuccessful in its mission and one of the crew survived."

"How do you know this, Kenna?" Olaf, her father's longtime friend and the village priest asked as he tugged on his long, white beard.

"Because I saw him." She closed her eyes and was immediately haunted by the brute's startling blue ones staring back at her.

"There were no bodies," Hamish said.

"There was one. You and Bryce had run off when I saw it in the waves. Why do you think I have only just returned to Tillicoulty? I stayed behind to investigate."

"You should have called us to come back." Hamish shook his head and his jaw tensed the way it always did when he was cross or frustrated.

"You should have followed your brother." Her father frowned deeper still.

Kenna paced to a table that held a jug of ale. She poured herself a mug then sipped. "If I hadn't stayed to investigate, we would be sitting here without the knowledge that one of them is out there, no doubt plotting how to steal from us, murder us, and burn down our village. I'd say it's a good job I stayed behind to investigate."

The council were quiet as they caught one another's gaze.

"Are you sure it wasn't just a body?" Olaf asked after a few moments.

"At first that is exactly what I thought." She took another drink, thirsty after her run. "So I flipped him over and checked for a heartbeat. But then…"

"Then what?" Her father was fiddling with the cross at his neck.

"Then he opened his eyes and stared at me—stared right through me with the look of a devil. In fact, I do believe I witnessed the Devil, right there on the beach. Oh, yes, he'd come straight out of hell."

There were a few gasps, and clicks of tongues.

"You were in mortal danger, child." Olaf glanced at her father. "We should give thanks to God that you are home safe."

"But for how long will home be safe?" Hamish asked, his hand going to the handle of the seax on his belt.

"Aye, he could be marching here now, following your footsteps," her father said.

"No, he seemed pretty messed up by the ocean." But even as she spoke, Kenna glanced at the door.

"Were there any others?" Olaf asked. "Or just him?"

"I only saw him, though to tell you the truth, I didn't hang around."

"There were no others," Hamish said. "Bryce and I would have seen them."

"Mmm," her father said, sitting bent over as though he needed all of his energy to think. "You're sure there's only one?"

"Yes. I'm sure."

"Then God may have had mercy on us if that is the case."

"It is the case, and I would bet coins that we will not see him tonight," Kenna said. "He was almost dead. It will take him time to regain strength. But I think on the morrow or the day after, he will appear, not least because I am sure he will be a good tracker."

"They are known for skill on sea and land," Hamish said, nodding seriously.

"So we must be ready," her father said. "With round-the-clock sentries on the gate and watchtower, all farmers in the confines of the village unless doing essential work."

"Which can be put on hold this time of year," Olaf said. "Mostly."

There was a murmur of agreement and general nodding.

"Hunting can go on, checking of traps, fishing and foraging," Olaf said. "That is essential and those men will have weapons with them. That will be our new law."

"Should we kill him on sight?" Hamish asked, the right side of his mouth curling up in a snarl.

Her father was quiet, head tipped, then, "No, I should like to know why he is here, how he found our wee corner in this land of Scots. Was it by accident or were we his destination?"

"By accident, I'd say," Hamish huffed. "His boat sank. Caught on the rocks at Clam Bay."

"Which means he's trapped on land," Kenna said. "Unless he faces the mountains in the east, which is unlikely, he will have to pass our village... No, he will have to go practically *through* our village. It is the only route to the low lands of the west."

A hush fell over the room. What she'd said was true. Unless God had other ideas and the castaway died of exposure overnight, they'd be seeing him soon.

KENNA SLEPT FITFULLY, plagued by dreams of the monster on the beach. His muscles had been so thick and solid, his weight dense when she'd moved him. The swirling tattoos from his jawline to his throat had been dark and intricate, and in her dream, the boar fang pendant had become a full set of gnashing jaws.

She tossed and turned, unable to get rid of the sense of being watched…*seen*…right to her core. He'd looked surprised. Behind the madness in his eyes, behind the evil, there had been a strange calmness.

That had unnerved her the most. The chillingly serene stare of a dead man looking into her soul.

"Kenna. Kenna. Wake up."

"Mmm?" She sat and blinked open her eyes to the dimly lit room.

Her mother stood before her. "Come and help me make bread."

"I have traps to check."

"Not today. Hamish and Bryce are doing them."

"But some of the traps are mine." She frowned and pushed back the covers, the cool air wrapping around her legs. "The catch will belong to me." Quickly, she pulled on pants, not caring that her mother would berate her for looking like a boy. It was cold and her gown was dirty. Next, she drew a short cloak around her shoulders, adding an extra layer over her woolen tunic, and pinned it with a round, silver brooch her grandmother had left her when she'd died. She pulled the hood up tightly.

"Feed the animals. There's swill there for the pigs," her mother said, frowning at her outfit but thankfully not commenting. "And once the fire is restocked, we'll cook eggs. Give us some strength before all that kneading, eh."

Kenna held back a retort. It was clear she'd been banned from leaving the village today. Much as it irked her, she'd been lucky not to get into more trouble for going on the beach and poking a Viking.

A few hours later, the fire had warmed the air and their small home smelled of baking bread and herby boar stew cooked in a broth thick with onions and turnips. They'd eat that later.

"The sentries have been doubled," her mother said, "because of your Viking."

"He's not *my* Viking."

"Your Norseman, then."

"No." Kenna set down the socks she was mending. "Whatever you want to call him, he's not mine."

"But you saw him." Her mother licked the end of her darn then studied the eye of a needle as she threaded. "It was only you who saw him."

"Don't you believe me? Don't you believe I saw a Viking?"

"Of course I do." She picked up a tunic that had lost its buttons. "I just remember when you said you'd seen a bear at the well that time."

"*Mother!*" Kenna stared at her, wide-eyed.

"And there wasn't one; you caused quite the fuss. The whole village was worried."

"I was eight years old, and Father had been filling my head with stories of bears. I wanted to see one."

Her mother didn't reply.

"I swear on the Holy Cross, yesterday, he was there on the beach, larger than life. A huge man, wet, covered in seaweed and sand. His hair was long and his neck…painted."

"'Painted'?"

"Aye, dark ink, black ink." She stroked her throat.

Her mother shuddered. "I hope I never see him."

"I wish for that too, Mother, for your sake."

They went back to darning quietly. The black-and-white dog, Lass, slept beside the fire and in the corner of the room one of the cats stalked a mouse.

Kenna let her mind wander. She thought how frightening it must have been to be aboard the vessel in the storm. How deafening it would have been when the hull had dragged and scraped on the razor-sharp rocks in Clam Bay.

Clam Bay was notorious. The people of Tillicoulty never launched from there—it was good only for collecting seafood. Just to the north was Eliah Bay, which was much easier to navigate from should the need to trade in one of the islands around Orc arise, though it didn't often. They had everything they needed here.

Lass pricked up her ears, then lifted her head. Her attention was set firmly on the doorway.

"What is it?" Kenna asked, continuing to stitch. "What can you hear?"

Lass barked.

The tabby cat darted behind a store of grain.

"Shh." Her mother looked up, nibbling on her bottom lip.

Kenna strained to hear. Aye. In the distance, there was a commotion. Shouting. A drum banged over and over. A warning.

Kenna's heartbeat rocketed. Her chest tightened and a rush of energy pulsed into her blood. "It's time," she said. "He's here."

"Lord have mercy." Her mother crossed herself then stood, the tunic falling to the floor.

Kenna stashed the sock aside and stood. "Should we go?"

"Aye. We need to be prepared." Her mother grabbed a pitchfork that was set beside a bale of hay. "We need to be prepared to battle for our lives if necessary. And remember, keep your legs closed and gauge out his eyes if you need to. God will forgive."

"Hopefully, it won't come to that. One of him and a village full of strong farming men. We will be victorious."

"I have heard of their superhuman strength and wily ways."

Kenna checked her dagger was on her belt then followed her mother out into the gray winter's day with Lass at her feet.

There was a tumult around the closed gate. A group of women held torches and pitchforks, their bodies steeled for an invasion.

"I'm going up to see what's going on," Kenna said, nodding at the ladder to the narrow rampart and watchtower. "See what the men are doing."

"No! What if he has a bow and arrow?"

"He doesn't, Mother. I saw him, remember?"

Kenna took off at a run, the dog at her heels. He'd arrived, as she'd known he would.

As she quickly climbed the ladder, she could make out men's deep voices. Tense. Irritated. Stern.

But they were all speaking in her language.

Perhaps it wasn't him.

Maybe King Athol had paid them a surprise visit.

She moved quickly to the watchtower with its small-pitched wooden roof and peered down.

It wasn't the king.

"Oh, dear Lord." She gripped the wooden rail. "He's not alone. There're more of them."

Standing grouped with their backs to each other were not one, but seven Vikings—six huge men and one flamed-haired woman who held a battered, round shield.

They were surrounded by village men who wielded pikes and pitchforks, but they looked small compared to the new arrivals. The farmers' eyes flashed with fear and uncertainty as they took in the Viking's long, sharp daggers, which thankfully were still safely attached to their belts.

"Who is your king?" A deep, accented voice.

"I am the village leader." Her father stepped forward, looking more hunched than usual despite his chin being tilted up bravely. "And who are you stepping onto on our land?"

"I am Haakon Rhalson, son of King Urd Rhalson of Drangar."

Kenna gasped and covered her mouth. It *was* him. And the brute she had seen on the beach, he was their leader.

"I suggest, Haakon Rhalson, that you continue on your way." Her father pointed west. "As you can see, we are not accustomed to unannounced visits and we have nothing to offer you."

Haakon shrugged and she saw the corners of his mouth tilt into a roguish smile as his eyes narrowed. "That's not very friendly, now, is it?"

"I'm not feeling friendly today," her father said. "It is the bleak depths of midwinter. We are surviving, nothing more."

"So how about a trade to brighten the gray?" Haakon said, pulling a small bag from his tunic pocket. "I have amber, lots of amber. We could do with food and mead and are willing to trade."

"'Trade'?" Her father shook his head in obvious confusion. "I thought the likes of you just took what you wanted."

Haakon threw back his head and laughed. It was a deep guffaw that seemed to shake the very walls of the fort.

Kenna gripped the wooden struts tighter and her toes curled in her boots. What was going on?

"Oh, I do," Haakon said, breaking out of the safety of his circle and ignoring the sharp pikes and pitches jabbing his way. He clasped her father's shoulder, his hand massive. "I *do* just take what I want."

Suddenly, he looked up.

His attention landed on Kenna.

She sucked in a breath. Frozen to the spot. He was staring at her with the same intensity he had the day before. His startling, blue eyes were otherworldly, keen, all-knowing.

But, for some reason, he too appeared frozen as the entire crowd watched him warily.

Then his lips curled into a slow smile again, and without breaking eye contact with her, he spoke. "But today, I am feeling generous and I am willing to trade peacefully with you good people. Because…well…let's just say there is something I want here that will require a little more delicate negotiation."

Chapter Nine

Two Hours Earlier

"OH, BLOODY HELL, in the name of the gods! Look! Is that what I think it is?" Astrid burst into a sprint, heading east along the shoreline.

Haakon paused, plucking mussels from a rock and watched her kicking up the sand.

"It is!" she yelled. "It's a shield from our boat."

When she reached the flat, circular object, she snatched it up and held it at arm's length.

"It's still strong," she called to him.

"Good." He nodded up the beach. "Let's go eat."

The others had also collected shellfish and they were now cooking on a hot rock beside the fire.

His stomach growled as the scent wafted toward him. Seaweed for supper hadn't suited him and he didn't intend for that to be his only option to eat on this night.

Astrid spun a circle, dancing with her shield, then she mocked a sword fight, twisting and turning and ducking.

Haakon laughed and exited the rock pools. Very little of their boat had washed up—a few planks, a part of the sail with a rope and strip of mast, and an empty barrel. But at least they all still had their daggers, clothes, and boots—something to be grateful for.

Egil was sat poking at the small morsels of food with a stick. "Got more?" he asked when Haakon approached.

"*Ja,* here." Haakon dumped a pile on the sand. "Wish we'd had more than a shield wash up. The sea has eaten everything we had."

"She's happy, though." Gunner nodded at Astrid.

"Always a good thing." Knud chuckled. "Her temper is like a snake's venom."

"I would agree with you there, my friend." Haakon sat on a low rock and let his wrists dangle over his bent knees. He watched Elgin start scraping the meat from shells.

"Mountains to the east," Ivar said, sitting opposite him and reaching for a cooked morsel of shellfish. "Not sure about west." He popped the food into his mouth.

"We'll head west," Haakon said.

"More chance of finding a village to raid or a boat to claim." Gunner nodded. "Good idea."

Haakon sighed.

"What?" Knud asked. "You don't think there'll be a village? There must be."

"I know there'll be one. We're not the first in this cave. Someone uses it regularly."

"True." Ivar glanced around. "Which is a good thing, right? We need stuff. Plus, we want a boat."

"But do we?" Haakon questioned.

"Do we what?" Ivar asked.

"Do we want a boat?" Haakon had spoken slowly and he looked at each of his men in turn.

"Of course we want a fucking boat," Astrid said, standing in the cave entrance, silhouetted by the winter light. "We're the wolves of the sea. We need to roam and check our territory."

"The stones." Haakon gestured at the pouch of runes on her belt. "They have spoken. This is a place to start a new life, learn afresh. The soil is fertile, the sea giving." He paused. "What if this is the place we're meant to stay?"

"Stay...? I think you mean *claim*." Gunner raised his eyebrows and snorted.

"*Ja*, that's what I mean." Haakon looked out to sea. It had been an omen that they'd landed here, he was sure of it. The gods did everything for a reason. The stones spoke only the truth. You just had to understand their language, as Astrid could. "I want to stay here. I'm sure we'll find a good place to farm, to settle. Put down roots."

Everyone was quiet.

"Isn't that why you jumped on board with me?" He swung his attention to Orm, who for once was sitting still and quiet, though he'd swiped fresh charcoal under his eyes, which made him look brooding and dark. "Huh? Isn't that why you leaped from our homeland onto my boat? Because you wanted a new start."

"It is true, brother. I set sail with you looking for a new life, away from our thieving, asshole brother and our father's undisguised hatred of me."

"So you agree this could be a good place."

"I guess." Orm shrugged.

"And that we should try to do this peacefully?" Haakon went on. "Negotiate with the locals rather than slay them."

"Why?" Knud said. "I don't understand."

"Because we could learn much from them, I am sure. Save ourselves years of figuring out how to farm this land for ourselves."

Orm thought for a moment. "I'm surprising myself when I say I think you might be onto something."

Haakon was quiet, but he raised his eyebrows at his brother.

Orm nodded. "*Ja*...so I am on board with trying the not-slaying-everyone plan. Count me in."

Haakon could have punched the air with triumph, but instead he kept the pleasure from his voice. "And you, Astrid?"

She banged her shield. "I will be peaceful until the first sword is raised against me, then I cannot be responsible for what I do. And I will pray the gods are with me."

Egil laughed. "I'm with Astrid because we're not going to find a welcoming committee. Even if we are like gods in comparison to these Lothlend people."

Haakon thought back to his Valkyrie on the beach. She'd been so beautiful. And she'd come to him again in his dreams, making him hard as he'd woken at dawn. That was very uncomfortable in damp breeches.

"This is all wrong. We should attack and talk afterward, when the men are dead or pleading for their lives," Gunner said. "After we've taken what loot we can find and satisfied ourselves with as many women as we can manage, then we talk."

Haakon nodded slowly and fought down the urge to assert his authority. "It's what we have done in the past. That is true."

"And it works well." Gunner gnawed on the inside of his cheek and stared at Haakon. He was a big guy, shoulders as wide as a bear, and the ground had been known to shake when he walked.

"That's true, when we are just passing by, then raiding is good," Haakon said. "But now we are staying…we want to, it is true, but also, we have no choice." He stood and stepped out of the cave. "We have no boat and no boat builder."

The hills to his right, though frosty, were not snow-covered and there was more light in the sky than he'd seen in weeks. "And I think we can flourish here. If this is what it is like in the depths of midwinter, imagine the long summer."

"Imagine if we can grow more than one season of crop." Knud rubbed his beard. "Two chances for a harvest rather than one."

"Do you think that could actually happen?" Egil asked.

"Why not?" Haakon felt enthused at the thought. "We've traveled south. The soil is more fertile, the weather less harsh and with more light…" He held his belly and laughed. "Why, we may all get so fat, we can't sail out of here for fear of sinking even the sturdiest boat."

There was a burst of laughter, partly because they were all so hungry, the thought of being so fat, they'd sink a boat became unusually funny.

"These look good," Astrid said, plucking up a cockle and blowing on it. "Well, *good*, as in they'll do."

Egil and Knud also started to eat.

Haakon looked toward the forest again. He squinted a little. There appeared to be a small track into the shadows. Perhaps that was the route used by the cave visitors.

When they'd eaten their forage, he'd suggest they follow it, see where it brought them out. It might just be the path of his destiny and lead him to the great riches he dreamed of: a farm, a family of his own, love, and respect.

HAAKON HELD UP his hand, signaling for his crew to stop. Instantly, their chatter silenced and they stood still, peering from the shadows of the pine forest. In the distance was a wooden fortress perched upon a shallow hill.

It was not unlike others Haakon had seen on his travels. Smaller, maybe, a few wooden sections in need of repair—a sign that the inhabitants didn't get bothered often by unwanted guests.

That enticed Haakon. A peaceful life was not wholly unappealing.

Smoke drifted upward in lazy spirals. There was little wind today after yesterday's storm. A couple of dogs barked their conversation.

"Look," Orm said. "They grow, even now."

Haakon's attention had already been captured by the rows of crops. Mostly, they weren't ones he recognized, strange, frothy leaves and flat, glossy foliage, tall sticks holding up winding greenery. A few villagers, dressed warmly, were tending the long, muddy rows.

A filthy pen held pigs who rooted around. Several horses were hogtied to prevent them from wandering and they munched on a pile of hay.

Several big fire baskets, alive with flames, lit the otherwise-gray day and were situated near to the animals.

"You never can get away from wolves and bears," Astrid said. "Those fires are a deterrent."

"*Ja*, I saw tracks back there. Wolves," Haakon said. "I also heard a raven's call. Odin is with us. He sees our every step."

"That is a good omen," Astrid agreed.

For a moment, they were quiet, watching the village. An ironsmith was at work, his hammer banging rhythmically against an anvil. The roofs that he could see were topped with frosty grass. Beside a gate—closed—stood four men holding pikes and a watchtower jutted into the gray sky.

"They're expecting us," Eglin said. "This doesn't seem like the type of place that usually has four guards."

"It's no surprise that we were spotted."

"Really?" Astrid said. "In that hellish storm, wouldn't you think these mice-like people would have been tucked up in their holes? Afraid of the wind and rain."

"'Haps they are hardier than you think." Orm shrugged.

"We were seen by locals." Haakon recalled the warm ashes and dropped nuts in the cave. "And now they're bracing for attack."

"Fuck it! I still say we should just raid." Gunner pulled out his long, glinting dagger. "Take what we want, decide who can live as our thralls and whores, and kill the rest."

Astrid banged her shield as though in agreement.

Haakon frowned at both of them. "We made a decision back there to do this peacefully."

"Those guards don't look too peaceful with their pikes." Astrid jerked her head their way.

"You blame people for wanting to protect their homes, their families?" Haakon said, raising his eyebrows. "Isn't that what we've always done back at Drangar?" He looked from Astrid to Gunner.

Gunner pressed his lips together and his nostrils flared.

Haakon studied the fortress again. The village within it was small. He'd guess maybe a hundred souls at most. They'd be self-sufficient too. This was a long way from anywhere and surrounded by mountains and bays full of cruel rocks. They'd *have* to be self-sufficient.

His guts clenched a little. Excitement? Anticipation? Had he found the place the gods had planned for him all along? He couldn't deny the spark of hope.

"They've got a church." Astrid spat on the ground. "They worship the one god, the way others have when we've raided west. How foolish are these people?"

"It's how they are, you know that." Haakon stepped from the shadows and into the weak winter light. "Come on, and keep your daggers sheathed unless I say otherwise."

He waited for Gunner or Astrid to object. They didn't.

As the warriors approached, the field workers spotted them and ran, minus their tools, toward the gates.

A sudden flurry and many men with pikes and pitchforks assembled, ready to defend as the gates were hastily closed, locking the women and children inside.

"They are braver than I thought," Orm said. "Most would cower within the walls. All of them."

"There are only seven of us. 'Haps that has given them courage," Astrid said.

"We are outnumbered, five to one at least." Gunner grunted. "Not that it's a fucking problem."

"Let us hope they speak the same language as my father's thrall." Haakon strode forward, shoulders swinging and chin tilted as he stepped over a small stream. "So we can negotiate."

"By 'negotiate,' you mean tell them what we want," Astrid said, already switching to the language of this land.

"Ja, that," he replied.

Haakon moved with purpose past the shivering crops and grazing horses toward the fortress.

"Halt! You are not welcome." A man stepped forward from the group of so-called guards. He had graying hair and a long beard, his fur cloak was dark, the hood pushed back, and he held a curved stick, much like Haakon's father's. His skin was like Urd's too. Weathered and wrinkled, sagging at the jowls, lined over his brow.

"We come in peace," Haakon said, holding up his hands, palms facing forward. He was glad they could understand each other. It made things much simpler.

"We don't want you here." For an old man, he had a commanding and strong voice. He flicked his head toward the forest. "Leave. Now."

"We need food and shelter. Our boat was smashed in the storm," Haakon kept walking. "We are stranded here. In this strange land."

"I *said*, halt." He banged his stick on the hard ground.

A dog ran up to Haakon, barking noisily, saliva hanging from its jaws as it circled. Haakon ignored it. A swift kick to the ribs would send it scampering if it got too brave with its teeth.

"Let us talk." Haakon stopped a few feet from the man who he presumed was their jarl.

The other men, crowded behind their leader, had their pikes and pitchforks at the ready and their expressions ranged from grim determination to obvious fear.

Haakon stood a head taller than all of them, heavier too. He was aware of Astrid to his right, Orm to his left. Gunner grunting behind him, and Eglin, Ivar, and Knud coming up the rear. He hoped they'd done as he'd instructed and kept their weapons holstered. They were intimidating enough as it was.

"We do not wish to fight or raid," Haakon said. "Or destroy your crops and homes."

"I do not believe you."

"*We* do not believe you," said a broad, young man with hair the color of a sunset on a hot day. He held an axe at his side and there was a silver cross around his neck, dangling from a slim, leather chain.

"You should believe." Haakon paused and glanced around. He spotted a well and a store of grain and logs. These people were organized for winter. "Who is your king?"

"I am the village leader. The *toisech*. And who are you stepping onto on our land?"

Haakon pulled in a deep breath. Proud as ever of his ancestry. "I am Haakon Rhalson, son of King Urd Rhalson of Drangar."

"I suggest, Haakon, son of King Urd Rhalson, that you continue on your way." The village leader pointed west. "As you can see, we are not accustomed to unannounced visits and we have nothing to offer you."

Haakon shrugged and a small smile tugged at his lips. It was as he'd suspected. This was an isolated village, which meant for peaceful times. "That's not very friendly, now, is it?"

"I'm not feeling friendly today," the leader said, raising his eyebrows. "It is the bleak depths of midwinter. We are surviving, nothing more."

Haakon pulled out a small bag from his tunic. He needed to show his intentions with actions rather than words. "So how about a trade to brighten the gray? I have amber, lots of amber. We could do with food and mead and are willing to trade."

"'Trade'?" The man's brow creased. "I thought the likes of you just took what you wanted."

Haakon threw back his head and laughed. Orm joined in, clapping and stamping his feet too.

The farmers with pikes angled their weapons at Orm. Clearly bemused by his reaction.

"Oh, I do," Haakon said, breaking out of the safety of his group and ignoring the sharp pikes and pitchforks pointed his way. He clasped the old man's shoulder. "I *do* just take what I want."

Suddenly, he felt eyes on him from above.

His attention strayed upward, to the watchtower above the gate, and landed on a beautiful woman with dark-brown hair that was catching on the breeze. She was studying him with an intensity that was as hot and wild as any flame.

His heart did a strange beat, a stutter, then an extra beat to catch up. His attention was glued on her. A hundred thoughts tumbled in his mind. His beautiful Valkyrie was here, right now, staring down at him.

And it wasn't because he was about to be killed, slain in battle, and escorted by her to Valhalla. No, it was because she was a real, living, breathing mortal, a woman—a woman he wanted in a way he'd never wanted anyone or anything before.

He smiled, keeping his attention firmly on her. "But today, I'm feeling generous and I am willing to trade peacefully with you good people. Because…well…let's just say there is something I want here that will require a little more delicate negotiation."

Chapter Ten

KENNA'S HAND FLEW to her mouth and she dropped down and out of view. What was he talking about? Not her... Surely, not her. He didn't want her.

Lass, who had managed to get up to the rampart, nuzzled his nose against her neck.

She tickled him between the ears, taking comfort in his familiar soft fur and his scent.

"What is it you want?" her father said. "Really?"

"My friend," Haakon said. "I want to converse with you, discuss your crops that I have never seen, your seasons, that is all. I told you, we come without plans of raiding or maiming. I even speak your tongue so that we can be civil."

"Men who are battle-scarred from fighting Scotsmen on Scot Land and bear arms against us," Hamish said firmly, "are not our friends."

Kenna peered over the top of the fortress again, one eye observing between two splintered, spiked poles.

"It is true: we are scarred and bear arms." The woman, with glinting, copper hair and a shield, stepped up to Hamish and stood with her feet hip-width apart. "You also have scars." She tilted her head and continued to study him. "I guess that shows we are like-minded." She reached out and touched his hair. "Not the only thing we have in common." She held his eye contact with a confidence that didn't fit her small stature as she spread the strands of his hair between her thumb and index finger.

"How do you speak our language?" Hamish asked her, his eyes narrowed and his shoulders tense. He didn't move away from her and his gaze settled on the wolf's head brooch that held her cloak secure. "You have come from across the sea. A foreign land."

"We have known your kind of people before." She dropped his hair with a dismissive flick of her fingers. "And we are particularly clever people when it comes to learning language." She chuckled and tapped her head. "We do, after all, have the gods on our side."

"Gods?" Hamish touched the strands of his hair she'd just held.

"You saw us?" Haakon asked, nodding at Hamish. "When our ship wrecked on the rocks."

"Aye." Hamish stood his ground. "But we didn't think anyone would survive. It was the kind of storm only the Devil himself could have created."

"The 'Devil'?" another Norseman asked, the one who had laughed and clapped. The one with kohl streaked down his cheeks. "Who is that? Who is your devil god?"

"The Devil is not a god, and he is someone I hope you do not turn out to be," her father said firmly. "I am Noah MacCallum, son of Jack MacCallum of Tillicoulty."

"That is the name of this place?" The flame-haired woman nodded at the fort gate. "Tillicoulty?"

"Aye, that it is. And the surrounding land and bays all belong to us."

Kenna watched with horror as her father, Noah, nodded to the guards. "Open the gates. We will feed and water these people. God has saved them from the wicked seas. We must do our part in seeing they are fit to go on their way." He swung to face Haakon, long cane outstretched and almost jabbing him on the chest. "Do not make me regret this, Haakon Rhalson."

"Oh, you won't." Haakon glanced upward again, as though he could look right through the wooden struts and see Kenna. "I will only bring satisfaction to your people. That is my promise."

Kenna gasped and sank low, hugging Lass tighter. What was Noah thinking letting these people into their home? They'd raid and murder, rape and pillage. The church would be emptied of what meager treasures they had, the crops destroyed, homes burned to ashes before nightfall. Animals slaughtered, women raped, and men sodomized.

They should kill them all now. She'd fight alongside her brother and the other strong, young men of the village. She could easily take on the woman with the long hair and the shield, she was sure of it.

There was clanking and movement below as the opening gates allowed entry into the village. She pressed her back to the wall and hoped she wouldn't be spotted.

Lass ran from her, then did her usual leap onto a low, grassy roof and down to the ground from there. She barked and ran in a circle as the group of Vikings entered the village.

It was clear the other men of the Tillicoulty were as skeptical as she. Their spines were stiff, their lips tight, flat lines. Bryce had wrinkled his nose, as though there was a bad smell around, and her father's friend Olaf, his cheeks were flushed and he held his Bible tight to his chest.

"You have good light," Haakon said, gesturing around. "For the season."

"Soon, darkness will spread and be here for many hours," Noah replied.

"In our northern land, it barely gets light each day. Only a sliver on the horizon."

"I have heard that. It sounds…depressing."

"It is a hard way to winter. Preparation is key."

They carried on walking, their conversation going out of Kenna's earshot. Inquisitiveness gnawed at her and she nibbled on her thumbnail. Was she brave enough to join the group after *that* look?

The second time he'd set his eyes upon her had been even more intense than the first. A shiver went up her spine at the memory and the same curiosity that had gripped her on the beach returned.

She saw Bryce and Hamish walking stiffly, flanking Noah, two guardian angels. She should have been there. She could fight as well as those two men she'd known since they'd been boys.

Quickly, she stood, brushed down her tunic and pants, and pushed her hair over her shoulders. With a straight back and her chin tilted, she headed for the ladder and quickly descended.

The ground was beginning to frost again, the meager heat of midday slipping into the shadows. She followed the group toward the Great House, her footsteps crunching the few blades of surviving grass.

She glanced upward. A crescent moon hung in the fading sky surrounded by slippery, gray clouds.

Bryce looked over his shoulder, saw her, and frowned.

"*What?*" she mouthed.

He flicked his hand. "Go away."

"No." She wouldn't be dissuaded. She was going with them.

Lass was around her legs now. Kenna tickled her between the ears and carried on walking.

"What is happening?" her mother asked, suddenly at her side and pulling a thick shawl around her shoulders. She still held the pitchfork, though its prongs were angled at the ground now.

"Father has invited the Vikings in to trade." Kenna tutted and shook her head. "This won't go well."

"At least no blood has been shed."

"Yet!"

Noah entered the Great House. The door was low, the shallow, conical roof covered in turf that had hibernated like everything else for the winter. A steady stream of smoke rose from the central chimney.

Haakon followed, hunching down to enter. His men and one woman went with him.

Soon, the other villagers and Vikings slipped from view. Kenna and her mother entered along with her aunt and young cousin. Lass waited outside, knowing she wasn't allowed in this building.

For a moment, Kenna paused in the shadows of the doorway, letting her eyes adjust to the dimness. This space was lit with tallow candles and a long fire trough. There were also fires hanging from iron baskets that were used for communal cooking and heat and light.

"Where is the mead?" Haakon asked, folding onto a bench and looking around as he sat. He ran his tongue over his lips.

Kenna edged backward, hiding herself between several seal skins hanging from hooks.

"Fetch our guests food and drink," Noah said, his voice not as deep and steady as usual.

Her father was nervous and he had good right to be.

"Plenty of it," the woman said, sitting and crossing her long legs. She jabbed the toe of her boot into the air as she also looked around. "Our stomachs think our throats have been cut."

The tall, lean Viking, the other one who had spoken their language, cackled and drew his finger across his throat as he lurched toward Olaf.

Olaf crossed himself and sat with a bump on a nearby straw bale.

"You have a church," Haakon said to her father.

"We are good, Christian people."

"Christian." He nodded slowly and pointed to the pendent cross lying over her father's tunic. "That is the Christian cross, am I right?"

"Aye." Her father touched it. "It is a sign of our faithfulness to the Holy Father."

"And your one lonely god has many treasures?" the woman asked, biting on her bottom lip as though holding in delight. "In your church?"

"Who are you?" her father asked.

"This is my sister, Astrid," Haakon said, scowling at her.

"What?" Astrid said. "I want many treasures to take to my afterlife. There is nothing wrong with that."

"We do not have treasures of gold and silver," Olaf said, shaking his head and still eyeing the tall Viking with streaks of black on his face. "We are not a rich village. Our treasure is but one dog-eared Bible and our faith in prayer." He paused. "A couple of iron candlesticks too."

"No silver and gold?" Astrid folded her arms tightly. "I don't believe you." She paused and pointed at Hamish's cross. "Because I see some there."

Hamish kind of *snarled* at her.

"You are welcome to search for treasure," Noah said. "Though you did agree not to raid, that we would feed and water you, trade with you, and then you would be on your way."

A tray of mugs was set on a table and the Vikings reached eagerly for the ale, glugging and grunting and shouting, *"Skål!"*

To Kenna, it sounded as if they were shouting "skull." Perhaps that was their toast for a collection of victims…victim's skulls.

"Ja, about that *being on our way* thing." Haakon took a deep slug of ale then rested the base of the mug on his thigh and sat back. He spun his gaze around the room, shadows flicking over his face. Then he pushed his hand through his hair, shoving it back over his head. One black strand fell forward, licking beside his right temple.

Kenna didn't know how he could exude such confidence in a strange land around strange people who clearly didn't want him there.

But he did. He had confidence in bucket-loads.

"Go on." Noah scowled at Haakon and sat, his cane between his legs and both hands curled over the top.

"We've decided to stay." Haakon held Noah's gaze. "Here. In your village."

"I don't fucking think so," Bryce said, withdrawing his long dagger and stepping forward, holding it menacingly in Haakon's direction.

"You've pushed your luck coming this far. Had I been village leader, you would have been dead just for looking upon our home."

In a sudden flurry of movement, the biggest of all the Vikings was in front of Bryce, his weapon also drawn and his eyes—partly hidden beneath thick eyebrows—flashing with menace and excitement. He said something sharp and guttural in a foreign language.

Haakon stood. He rested his hand on the shoulder of his companion. "Sit, Gunner. We agreed to negotiate."

Gunner, tall and bearded, didn't move.

"I said, *sit*," Haakon said again, gruffer this time.

Gunner hesitated then sat heavily on a straw bale. He didn't take his angry gaze from Bryce as he gnawed on a hunk of bread and chewed with his mouth open.

"You can't stay in our village." Noah's lips pursed. "This is our home, not yours."

"I never said it couldn't be your home." Haakon raised his eyebrows. "I am simply saying it will be ours too."

"But... But why?" Olaf said.

"Go back to your own land, where you belong." Hamish jerked his thumb over his shoulder. "All of you." He'd directed the last words at the woman, Astrid.

"We don't want to." She shrugged. "And I don't do anything I don't want to do."

"Or you *can't*." Hamish raised his eyebrows at her. "Now that you don't have a boat and you don't know how to build one."

"It is complicated," Haakon said. "For my father is king."

"And he does not want his son at his side?" Noah asked, raising his eyebrows.

"He does not want *all* of his sons at his side." Kohl-Faced Viking clasped his fist down on a walnut, smashing it and sending bits of shell skittering off the table.

"You should explain," Noah said, swallowing loudly then brushing a splinter of shell from his sleeve.

"I do not have to, old man." Haakon took another slug of ale, seeming to drain his mug. "But I will." He cleared his throat and once again surveyed his rapt audience. "My father is king. My twin brother and I were both in line for the throne. We both wanted the throne. So we did the only thing that seemed fair: we fought for it."

"And you lost," Bryce said with a note of pleasure in his voice. "You lost the crown." He chuckled.

"'Haps you are right." Haakon held his mug out for more ale.

The carpenter's wife quickly filled it.

"Or it is simply the path the gods have planned for me," Haakon went on. "All-seeing Odin works in mysterious ways and I saw his raven on my way here, just today." He lowered his voice. "I believe the gods took the crown from me so that I would move onto better lands, with fertile soil, generous seasons. My destiny is so much bigger than my brother Ravn's. More prosperous, more satisfying, more of everything." He stood as though warming to his subject. "I will wear the crown of a superior land. I will be richer." He paused and laughed suddenly. "And fatter—and so will my crew." He held his belly and thrust his hips forward.

Kenna's eyes widened.

Gunner stopped glaring at Bryce and suddenly laughed. He spoke in his native tongue and his friends chuckled.

"You think we are your destiny?" Noah asked, holding his brow as though his head ached. "Tillicoulty?"

"*Ja*, it makes sense. My life was spared not once but twice during a battle with my brother and then at sea. And then…then I wash up on a beach, believing myself to be dead and what do I see?" He bit on his bottom lip and looked around, his eyes searching.

The room seemed to hold its breath as one.

Kenna's heart clattered up against her ribcage. She pressed deeper into the shadows.

"I will tell you what I saw." Haakon took a step away from his group. Past her father, past Olaf and Hamish, and looked straight at the seal skins. He nodded slowly, his mouth tipping into a hint of a smile. "As I lay there thinking of the Great Hall in Valhalla and the feasts the divine chef Andhrímnir would prepare me each day, I saw my Valkyrie. She had come to take me to the next realm."

He took a step closer to Kenna and she clasped her hands beneath her chin. "God help me."

"Except…" Haakon went on. "She was no Valkyrie. No vision. No dream. She was real, as real as the day I was born and the most beautiful woman I have ever laid eyes upon." He came close still, until he was but a few feet from her.

"Mother," she gasped as his eye contact glued onto hers.

"Oh, heaven help us." Her mother crossed herself.

"So beautiful that I could not breathe," he went on, "that my heart stopped and then started again, started again with only her in it." He swiped his tongue over his bottom lip. "She is whom I've waited my whole life for."

Kenna whimpered. This couldn't have been happening. This was sheer madness. Insanity. A devilish trick.

But then in one quick movement, Haakon reached for Kenna's hand, and with a strong grip, he pulled her from the dark edge of the Great House.

"Oh! Please. No," she cried.

"I saw in that moment," he boomed over her protesting voice, "that my destiny was here. I saw the woman who will become my wife. Even if you already have a husband, I will kill him so I can claim you." He paused. "Do you have a husband?"

"She does not," someone in the crowd called out.

Kenna glared at the meddling old woman who had added to her predicament.

"Good." Haakon grinned. "And so, this woman, this beautiful

woman will bear the fruits of my seed from her womb and give me many heirs to my new land."

He yanked her closer still so that she was forced to clutch his arm for balance.

"Your wife?" Noah stood and banged his cane on the floor. "That is my daughter. She will not bear you heirs. She will not bear heathen children. I forbid it."

"No, please, no." Kenna's mother rushed forward. "I beg you. She is but a child."

"'A child'?" Haakon caught Kenna's chin in his hand and stared into her face. "A *child* of more than twenty summers, I'd bet."

"Get the hell off me." She twisted from him, but he kept his arm wound around her waist, dragging her body close to his.

"And I think you should think twice before forbidding me anything that I desire," Haakon said, focusing on Noah. "Because one word from me and my men will kill your entire village with barely a scratch landing on their flesh."

Chapter Eleven

A STRID SNARLED AND banged her shield, as though confirming Haakon's threatening words. Orm tossed his dagger into the air, let it spin three times, then caught it neatly. Gunner growled and Egil, Ivar, and Knud followed suit and bared their teeth.

Haakon looked around the crowded room. A sea of faces was turned to him and each held fear in their eyes.

Good. If they were scared, intimidated, then perhaps blood wouldn't be shed.

"Kenna is my daughter," Noah said. "*I* decide who she marries."

"Then you should decide upon me." Haakon banged his fist on his chest, letting the name *Kenna* settle there. It was a beautiful name and one he'd waited his whole life to hear. "Because if you do, I will not kill you and your people."

Noah's mouth hung open as he stared first at Kenna and then the other old man someone had called Olaf.

"You said you would come in peace," Olaf said, as though speaking for his leader. "And now you wish to pleasure yourself with our *toisech*'s only daughter?"

"I wish to *marry* this woman, Kenna, daughter of Noah Mac-Callum. *Ja.*" He paused. "If I sought only pleasure, I would take her out to a barn right now, tear off her pants, and satisfy myself as though she were nothing but a mead wench." Though that idea wasn't totally unappealing. Kenna smelled nice, like flowers—lavender, perhaps. A stark contrast to how he smelled, Haakon knew that.

"Get off me, you big, ugly brute." Kenna shoved at him, pushing him hard in the ribs with the heels of her hands.

He didn't budge. "I dare say you think I am as ugly as I think you are beautiful."

"Do not speak of me that way. I don't want to be your wife." Her nose wrinkled, confirming his smell was distasteful.

"But I am the new… What do you call it? Ah, yes, *toisech*. I am the new *toisech*, so you will obey me," Haakon said.

"I will obey my father." Again, she twisted. "He is the village leader. Not you."

Haakon held her tightly. She wasn't going anywhere.

"And she is my sister." The young man who had hair the color of Astrid's stepped up to Haakon. His eyes flashed with daring and his pale, freckled cheeks had flushed pink the same way Astrid's did when she was really angry about something. "I demand you let her go."

"I will let her go when it is agreed that we will wed."

"'Wed'? '*Agreed*'?" Kenna glared up at him. "Are you mad?"

"Probably." Oh, she was so pretty—her features petite and perfect, her mouth so kissable and her eyes brimmed with every emotion he wanted to learn more about. "But being mad means nothing can stop me from getting what I want. It means I am *very* determined." He leaned closer and spoke against her ear. "And I want you. Have from the moment you touched me on the beach. Do you remember that? Do you remember how you touched me and brought me back to life?"

She gasped and pulled away again.

This time, he let her stand free. He placed his hands on his hips and looked around the room. "So it is decided. My friends and I are staying in Tillicoulty, it is ours now, but because we are benevolent, kind men…" He pressed his hand to his chest and inclined his head. "We are not interested in killing—at this moment in time at least—instead, we wish to integrate. To marry your women, farm your fertile land,

and learn your skills."

Orm swung his arm around, pointing at everyone. "We wish to suck your knowledge from your brains." He laughed wildly. "And we wish to have our cocks sucked too." He made wild, swinging movements with his hips. "Oh, *ja*, baby!"

There were several gasps and a few women shrank deeper into the shadows.

Haakon wasn't sure if the villagers were more scared of him or Orm. His younger brother was more manic than usual today and with his wild hair and the charcoal on his face, he could have come straight from an underworld party with Loki.

"Father." Kenna made a cross shape on her chest. "Please, you can't let this brute become my husband."

Noah was quiet.

As were the other village elders.

"Father," Hamish said. "You can't really—"

"It is not going to happen," a young man with curly, dark hair said sharply as he withdrew his dagger. "I will not let it."

Haakon studied him. He was of average height. Had all of his teeth, though his nose looked as though it had been broken a couple of times. He was broad and strong, no doubt a decent hunter and with an eye for a bow and arrow. He also concluded that this man had affections for his wife-to-be.

Which made him an enemy amongst enemies.

"And who is going to stop it happening?" Haakon stepped up to him. "You?"

"Aye. I am Bryce O'Blaine of Tillicoulty. I will not let you marry Kenna."

"And why is that?" He paused. "Because you want to?"

Bryce's eyes darted to Kenna and his mouth opened. He didn't speak.

In that moment, Haakon knew that indeed, Bryce O'Blaine was in love with his bride. He chuckled. "Look at her all you want, boy, but she's mine now."

"No, I won't have it." Suddenly, Bryce lunged at Haakon with his blade.

Haakon dropped his body weight and sliced his forearm to the side, knocking Bryce's attack to the left and sending the dagger skittering over the floor. It came to a halt beside a barrel. He reached out and caught the young man around the throat, squeezing his fingers until he could feel his windpipe.

Bryce gasped and flailed his arms, going up onto his toes.

"I should kill you," Haakon snarled. "As warning to anyone else here who tries to stop me from getting what I want."

"Please, don't hurt my friend." Kenna was suddenly at his side, her small, warm hands curled over his tense forearm. "He is showing loyalty, that is all, and loyalty is not to be punished."

Haakon relaxed his grip. "Loyalty to whom?"

"To me, to the village, to his people. It is a good trait." She tugged. "He will not cause any more trouble."

"Is that right?" Haakon dragged his attention from Kenna's mouth and the way it moved as she spoke. "He won't cause any more trouble?" He studied Bryce, who had gone quite red and whose eyes bulged.

"Please. I beg you," Kenna said frantically.

Haakon released Bryce and pushed him away.

He stumbled backward and knocked into a barrel. Two villagers rushed to support him.

"I don't want to hurt anyone," Haakon said, stomping to the table and retrieving his ale. "I wish to live peacefully on the path of my destiny. Do not stop me from doing that."

"Please," Noah said. "Let us continue our negotiating tomorrow. You are tired from a long journey and the night is drawing in. Stay here, in our Great House, and rest, eat, and drink. Tomorrow, we will speak again."

"*Ja*, we will." Haakon sat. "There is much to discuss, except for one thing." He used his mug to point at Kenna. "I'm marrying her. Tomorrow. Before the light leaves the day, we will be man and wife and I will take the head of anyone who steps in my way."

"A wedding, such fun." Orm hopped onto a straw bale, his drink in hand. "Now leave, everyone. We wish to get our beauty sleep." He flicked his free hand toward the door. "And so do you." He cackled and pointed at Bryce. "Especially you, for you fell out of the ugly tree and hit every branch on the way down."

"Why, you..." Bryce cleared his throat and stepped forward, hand on his dagger handle.

Hamish gripped him. "He's not worth it. Leave it."

But Orm wasn't listening. He was at the barrel pouring ale and he had half a fish tail hanging out of his mouth. Not a care in the world, apparently.

Haakon sought out Kenna. She was with her father now as the anxious crowd moved with haste to the door.

She turned and glared over her shoulder at him, then lifted a small cross that hung around her neck and kissed it.

What did that mean? That she wanted to kiss him? That she was kissing her god?

He didn't know, but tomorrow, he would start asking her all the questions until he knew everything and had nothing left to unpick about her.

"You really want to marry that foreign woman?" Astrid said with a frown as Kenna disappeared from view.

"*Ja*, I do."

"Why?"

He sat. "Haven't you seen her? She's fucking beautiful." He closed his eyes, picturing her face again. "So beautiful."

"I guess, for a Lothlend woman, she has a certain prettiness."

Astrid shrugged. "Bet she can't fight, though. No shield-maidens here."

He opened his eyes and frowned. "She doesn't need to be able to fight." A surge of protectiveness came over him. "Not now I have arrived. I will ensure nothing ever harms her. Not one hair on her head."

"Fuck, you've got it bad, brother." Astrid frowned at him, a hint of confusion, or maybe disbelief, in her eyes. "Freya has rolled your destiny hard and fast."

"Didn't you say, when you read my rune stones, that the symbol of Ingwaz meant fertility?"

"*Ja*, brother."

"Well, don't you see?" He grinned suddenly and cupped his cock over his pants. "I have found the mother of my children. It is about time I started producing heirs to take over my new kingdom."

Astrid raised her eyebrows. "I am not sure how pleased she is going to be about your plan. She seemed particularly unamused by the prospect of being your wife. Do you really want a woman who is unwilling?"

"I will win her around."

"Ha," Orm said, slapping Haakon on the back. "She looked at you with daggers in her eyes. I am surprised you are not bleeding all over."

"*Ja*, watch your cock. She'll bite it off," Gunner said with a laugh.

Haakon frowned at him. "She'll be wet as spring rain and as willing as my most faithful horse by the time I have seduced her."

"'Seduced her'? Really? I'd like to see you try." Astrid poured ale and took a pickle from an earthenware pot. "You have about as much charm in you as a stupid giant."

"I have charm." Haakon was offended. "Have I not had women before? Many women?"

"True, but they just wanted to fuck the son of the king, did they not?" Orm said with a teasing smile. "Ride your big, pierced cock."

Haakon clenched his fists and resisted the urge to knock the smile off his brother's face. "Shut up or I'll banish you from my new lands."

Orm chuckled and bit into an apple. Juice squirted onto his chin.

Haakon, still frowning, looked around. "This will be our home now. It is a good size and warm. The roof looks solid."

"Beats the cave," Knud said.

"Ah, it's nice, even more so 'cause we didn't have to build it." Gunner threw a log into the fire trough.

"We'll divide it up with the wooden planks I saw piled up outside," Haakon went on, "make seven bedrooms."

"Might only need six," Egil said with a shrug.

"Why? Where are you going?" Haakon asked.

"Nowhere." He nodded at Astrid. "But I reckon she wants to get into the bed of that guy she was sparring with. The one with hair as red as hers."

"What!" Astrid who had sat on a bench, jumped up and clasped her dagger. "No way. Take that back. I wouldn't lie with one of these people. He's not even a warrior."

A rumble of mirth went around at her indignation.

"You did seem quite taken with him," Haakon said.

"Imagine the children you'd have," Orm said. "Be able to see them in the dark."

"Why you—"

She swung a punch Orm's way, but he dodged it, knocking into a pitcher of water and sending it sliding over the table.

"Haakon may have lowered his standards, but I have not." Astrid glared at Orm and then at everyone else.

"Hey, I can't help it if the gods have chosen a woman from another land for me." Haakon shrugged. Nothing could shake him from his elevating mood. He'd found a new kingdom, a wife, and a home, and he had food, fire, and drink that he hadn't had to provide for himself for once. Life was good.

AFTER FEASTING AND making merry, Haakon and his crew created haphazard beds of straw and sacks. They'd fix up their new home tomorrow.

He slept well and was woken by the sound of a cockerel. His stomach rumbled and he hoped there were eggs and fresh bread to be had. It was then he remembered it was his wedding day.

Sitting up with a smile, he looked around at the other sleeping men. Orm was on his back snoring and Gunner let out a rumbling fart as he turned over. Astrid wasn't there and he guessed she'd gone hunting for food. She always woke starving.

He had to make a start on creating a bedchamber for his bride. He'd have the largest, naturally, in the back corner, and he'd set two chairs outside the door for them to receive visitors. The place was big enough that it could still be used for entertaining, for making judgements and doling out new laws. *Ja*. It would do nicely once his vision for it had been achieved.

He got up, drank from a jug of ale, then went outside into the chilly air to relieve himself.

It was early light. The small, round houses held a frosty glow.

A dog barked. The cockerel called again.

But other than that, all was quiet.

He studied the treeline, mainly evergreen firs. A few had ravens sitting on the top branches. He liked that; they were a good omen. Odin was watching over him as he set out on his new life. He'd learn and work hard, create something special to leave here on Earth when he went to the next realm. Something to be proud of.

He moved between the houses quietly. Smoke was seeping from several chimneys and sure enough, he could smell bread. A pen of pigs snuffled around hoping he'd throw them treats, but he had nothing.

His attention was caught by movement behind him and he turned and saw an older woman at a well. She glanced at him then quickly looked away, hunching over, as though trying to make herself invisible.

Haakon frowned and walked over to her. He wanted the villagers to fear him if they wronged him, but not as they went about their daily chores.

"I will do it," he said, reaching for the length of rope that held the pail.

She stared up at him with wide, green eyes lined with weathered skin.

"Here." He handed her the bucket. "Have a good day."

She made a strange, whimpering sound that caught in her throat, then scuttled away like a scared beetle.

"What are you doing?"

He spun around at the sound of a young woman's voice. And when he did his mouth stretched into a smile. "Bride, I bid you good morn." He gave a mock bow.

"I am not your bride." Kenna slammed her hands onto her hips and flattened her mouth. The black-and-white dog at her side sat and glared at him. Its ears pricked forward.

His heart seemed to swell in his chest. In the pale light, Kenna was even more beautiful. Fresh as newly fallen snow. A vision he'd never forget.

"And I never will be your wife." She tilted her chin.

"You do not have a choice." He pointed to the sky. "The gods have made it our destiny to be man and wife."

"The *gods*." She huffed. "What are these gods? I know of only one, the Holy Father, God Almighty, and you...Haakon Rhalson, are a heathen, and as such, you are not a man I can marry. Not ever." She tossed her hair over her shoulder. "So get that into that thick skull of yours and leave us be."

Chapter Twelve

KENNA HAD WATCHED Haakon help old Mistress Knowles at the well, seen him act with patience and kindness. It had surprised her and she'd rubbed her eyes to make sure she wasn't still asleep and dreaming.

But no, the chill air caressing her cheeks and neck and the brisk scent of frost told her she was wide awake.

"My skull might be thick," he said, pacing up to her and ignoring the dog's growl. "But my determination is steely, and you"—he caught her chin in his palm—"will be my wife by nightfall."

She stared up into his eyes and tried to beat down the coil of fear in her belly. He was so damn big, and wild, and strong. "I cannot marry you. It is not I who is refusing. It is God's will that we do not."

"It is *my* gods' will that we do."

She closed her eyes and reached for her cross.

He released her chin and his eyebrows drew together.

She kissed her cross.

"What is that?"

"It is the cross that Jesus Christ, our savior, was nailed upon to save us from our sins."

"Sins? What is 'sins'?" His eyebrows pulled together.

"An immoral act, shameful in the eyes of divine law." She swallowed tightly and held his eye contact. "It would be a sin for me to marry a man who does not have my God in his heart."

"Ah, so this is the problem."

"It is more than a problem; it is a divine obstacle." She took a step back. "One that cannot be overcome, so you must, Haakon, go and find another wife, one who has your gods in her heart, because I could never love another God. There is only one Holy Father. That is set out in the commandments."

Haakon gnawed on his bottom lip and appeared deep in thought.

Kenna wished the cockerel would shut up; it was in full swing now just behind her.

"Kenna!" Hamish appeared from a doorway of a small roundhouse. "Get back in here."

"We are speaking of important matters," Haakon said.

Hamish pushed his hand through his mussed-up hair. His breath plumed in front of his face. "Like what?"

"Your sister declares she cannot marry me because I do not have your god in my heart."

Hamish was quiet and Kenna sent a quick prayer heavenward that he would support her argument.

"Ah, I see." Hamish nodded. "My sister is right, for it is true you have never been baptized."

"'Baptized'?"

"Aye, a sacred act to show you have turned from your old life of sin to a new life with Jesus Christ."

"Who is this Jesus Christ?" Haakon looked around. "I should meet with him at once. Where is he?" He pointed to the carpenter's home. "Does he live there?"

"Jesus, please forgive us." Kenna raised her face to the gray sky. "For the heathen we have allowed into our village."

Haakon looked upward, as though expecting to see Jesus above him.

"You cannot meet with him on Earth," Hamish said. "He died for us. He now resides in heaven."

"Heaven." Haakon paused. "Ah, yes, I have heard of this. It is like

Valhalla."

"It is nothing like Valhalla." Kenna bristled. Not that she'd heard of Valhalla, but she was sure Valhalla would be a mead-swilling, whore-filled, overindulgent festival that couldn't have been more different to a peaceful and pure heaven.

Haakon shrugged. "I can be baptized. What do I have to do? Sacrifice something? Then there will be no stopping our marriage today."

Kenna's heart flipped. That was not what she'd been expecting him to say. "What? No...you can't... I..."

"It is not that simple," Hamish said. "You have to let God into your heart, so that He exists in your very soul."

"I can do that." Haakon spread his big hand over the leather tunic he wore. "In fact, I believe He is here already."

"You blaspheme," Kenna said with a shake of her head.

"I will do whatever I need to." He winked at Kenna. "To make you mine."

She scowled at him. "It is impossible for you to be baptized today."

"I can assure you it is not. Tell me what it entails." Haakon gestured to Hamish.

"Well...you..." Hamish glanced at Kenna. "You have to go to the bay, swear you forsake all gods except for God Almighty and that you will live as a Christian from this day on."

"Why the bay?" Haakon frowned and placed his hands on his hips.

"You must be naked and dunked under the water so that your sins are washed away and you are reborn," Kenna said. "And it is very cold."

"I know the water is cold." Haakon chuckled. "I was in that very ocean just yesterday, if you remember."

"And our priest, Olaf, will have to consent to perform the ceremony," Hamish went on.

"Did I hear my name?"

Kenna turned and saw Olaf and her father standing together. They each had worry lines plowed into their brows.

"Olaf." Haakon stepped up to him and whacked him on the shoulder in greeting. "Just the man I need to speak with."

Olaf staggered to the right and stared up at Haakon. "I feared as much."

"You will baptize me now. At the bay. So that Kenna does not fear she is marrying a… What did you call me? A heathen." He spun his hand through the air as though hurrying up the process of baptism. "And then we will marry. I will call her 'wife' and she will call me 'husband' by nightfall."

"Lord, give us strength"—Noah set his gaze upon Kenna—"to follow the right path. Lord, give us wisdom to do what is best. Dear Lord, have mercy upon us."

She knew what he was saying, that she must marry Haakon. He'd said it the night before too, as they'd eaten supper and argued. He'd said it over and over that she must do the Viking's bidding in order to save the village and all of the villagers' lives. For if she were stubborn and bloody-minded, as she tended to be on occasion, there would be many lives lost.

"Father." Kenna frowned at him.

"Kenna," Noah said. "Haakon has seen the light. He is willing to denounce his gods and put his faith in the Holy Father. That should be commended."

"But—"

"The bay is this way," Olaf said. "And as the sun is fresh in the sky, a new day dawns with the potential for redemption and unwavering service to God."

"To the bay." Haakon grinned and rubbed his belly. "I will eat upon my return."

"What are you doing?" Orm appeared, Gunnar at his side.

"I am being baptized," Haakon said. "Apparently, it is a requirement of my bride."

"She's got you wrapped 'round her littlest finger already?" Orm cackled and wriggled his pinkie at Haakon.

Haakon shrugged and said something in his native language. He then cupped his groin and looked at Kenna.

She rolled her eyes and turned away. But the moment she did, she was aware of a big hand wrapping around hers.

"Come, bride, come and watch. I do not wish you to have any doubts of my commitment to you and this marriage."

"I have no interest in watching." She tried to pull away, but he kept his hold tight. "This is a sham baptism. You know nothing of the Bible or God and our savior, Jesus Christ."

"'Haps not, but as your priest said, this is a new dawn and anything is possible." He started to walk toward the fortress gate, following Olaf, Noah, and Hamish.

Kenna had no choice but to trot at his side, taking two steps to each of his one.

Soon, Eliah Bay came into view. Like Clam Bay, it was a horseshoe shape with soft sand lined by pine forest. The water sparkled in the crisp dawn light and two small fishing boats bobbed against a wooden pier.

"I like this," Haakon said as they stepped onto the sand. "And your boats are…"

"They are what?" Kenna tutted.

"They appear small but seaworthy."

"Naturally. For sometimes, we visit the outer islands for trade."

"What do you trade?"

"Why do you want to know?"

"I am the ruler here now. I need to know everything." He grinned at her. A cocky, smug grin that made her want to slap his face.

"Come," Olaf said, removing his boots. "To the water's edge. You must be naked. You are being cleansed of all sins, of which I am sure there are many."

"Oh, dear Lord." Kenna screwed up her eyes. Really? She had to witness this? This was surely the worst morning of her life.

"Open your eyes," Haakon demanded.

"No." She pressed her lips together.

"*Ja*. Or my dagger will taste blood, right here, right now. I swear in the name of Odin…" He cleared his throat. "In the name of God. If you don't open your eyes, I'll…"

Kenna didn't want him to finish the sentence, so she opened her eyes and stared up into his. She hoped he could see the hate in them.

He didn't appear to and held up their joined hands. "You will stay here and watch. If I discover you have closed your eyes or you have slipped away, the baptism will be repeated. It is something you *will* witness."

Kenna scowled. "Are you always this bossy?"

"*Ja*." He laughed and released her hand. "So get used to it."

She stepped back as he bent his arm over his head and fisted his tunic between his shoulder blades. He drew it off and tossed it aside. It landed on a piece of driftwood.

The pale winter light caressed his muscular torso, dipping into each rise and fall of his abs and pecs. The boar fang hung to his sternum, tapping against his scribble of dark chest hair that started where his neck tattoo ended.

Next came his leather boots, also flung toward the driftwood and spraying up sand. His feet were pale, his toes long. After that, he shoved at his woolen pants, pushing them down his legs and kicking them away.

Kenna gasped and clutched her cross.

"You like what you see?" he said, standing straight and placing his hands on his hips. "I have a good cock, a king's cock. You are a lucky woman, Kenna."

"You… You are a monster." She swallowed tightly, her throat feeling stuffed full of dry bread all of a sudden. His thick cock hung from a patch of dark hair and even flaccid, it was of eye-watering size. The skin of his shaft was darker than the rest of his body and something glinted from the tip.

She peered a little closer, feeling the blood drain from her cheeks. She clasped her hand to her mouth to hold in a gasp of horror.

He chuckled. "Don't worry. You will be up close and personal with this mighty beast very soon."

"What... What is *that?*" she asked as the sun glinted off what appeared to be a metal ring in the end of his cock.

"It was a gift from my mother when I was fifteen summers," he said. "It adds to a woman's pleasure. She was a very thoughtful woman."

"Lord have mercy," Noah whispered, crossing himself. "I will pray for you, dear daughter."

"She will not need your prayers." Haakon fisted his cock and tugged the ring with his other hand. "For I will take care of her every need."

"We should...get on with this..." Olaf said, rolling up his trousers and exposing skinny, pale ankles. His face was pale too.

"Indeed." Haakon released his cock and strode down the beach.

His ass was high and tight, dimpled at each side, and another tattoo, of a snake, wound its way up his back. He had a scar on the back of his right leg, long and jagged, a little red.

A strange, fizzing sensation took hold of Kenna's belly. It sparkled around her body, making her breasts tingle and her pussy clench. What had this warrior man seen during his lifetime? Where had he traveled? What did he know that she did not?

All of these questions and more bounced around her brain and she hugged herself, holding everything in tight.

Haakon strode into the freezing water without flinching and soon he was waist deep. "Now what?"

Olaf stood on the water's edge, the waves tickling his ankles. Had it been summer, he'd have been deep, but clearly, he wasn't feeling up to the icy chill. "May the Devil be expelled from you. May ye now go into all the world!" he shouted, holding up his right hand and making the sign of the cross. "And preach the gospel to every creature. He who believeth and is baptized shall be saved. From this moment on, you must denounce all but the real God and worship only his son, Jesus Christ, who died for our sins." He paused and looked up at the sky. "Haakon Rhalson, son of King Urd Rhalson of Drangar, I now pronounce you Christian with the new Christian name of Rory." He looked back at Haakon.

"New name?" Haakon scowled.

Kenna was pretty certain he wouldn't go along with that plan. It was the disregard in his eyes and the quiet huff in his voice that told her he'd never answer to Rory.

"Aye, and now you must submerge yourself completely and be cleansed of all other gods and all of your sins."

Haakon didn't hesitate. He dropped down, low, his head disappearing beneath the waves.

All around her, Noah, Hamish, Gunnar, and Orm seemed to hold their breath. The moment went on and on. He didn't appear. The waves lifted and dropped.

Kenna looked out at the water, wondering if he'd pop up somewhere else.

But he didn't. After what felt like the longest time, he burst upward, shaking his head and flicking his hair from his face. He blew out a cloud of breath, which was instantly taken on the northerly wind.

"Amen, amen," Olaf called. "I say to you, no one can enter the kingdom of God without being born of water and Spirit, and on this day, Haakon Rhalson, you are born again as a Christian, as Rory, and we welcome you to our fold."

"What in the name of Thor is going on?"

Astrid's voice came from a few feet behind Kenna. She turned.

"What is going on?" Astrid asked again, storming to the sea edge and pointing at Haakon.

"Your brother is now a fellow Christian," Noah said. "The baptism has been performed."

"What? No, he isn't." Astrid's eyes were wide and her arms lifted high. "He is a loyal follower of the All Father and Thor and Freya. He understands how we wait for Ragnarök, how we must appease our gods with gifts and sacrifice and—"

"It cannot be undone," Olaf said. "And I don't believe he wants it to be."

Haakon strode from the water, his flesh shining and the waves breaking around him.

Kenna swallowed the strange taste of anticipation, hating that a part of her admired Haakon's obvious strength and virility. There was no man in the village to match him, not even Bryce or Hamish—though she was sure both men would object to that considerably.

"You bloody idiot!" Astrid stomped up to him, finger wagging. "What have you done?"

"I have done what my bride desires." He grinned. "I've been baptized."

"You have become a Christian. You have turned your back on the gods. You have invoked the anger of all the gods. Odin will never forgive you. You will pay for this. Their fury will know no bounds, crazy brother of mine." She twisted her finger by her ear. "You have been addled by desire. Fooled by a pretty face. You are so fucking weak and stupid—"

He reached out and snatched her wrist, his smile dropping. "Do not speak of me that way, for it is I who is leader here. It is I who has found us new lands, a new home. Show some respect."

"The way you respect Thor, Odin, and Freya?" She snorted. "You have brought shame upon our family." She withdrew from his grip. "You are no brother of mine."

Haakon's heavy eyebrows pulled low. "Astrid."

She let out a strangled squeal and stomped over the sand, only to be quickly swallowed by the forest.

Haakon pushed his wet hair back from his forehead. Streams of seawater trickled down his torso to his legs and his matted body hair held sparkling droplets. A lick of seaweed clung to his right calf muscle.

"Your clothes," Hamish said, holding out Haakon's pants. "Cover up, for God's sake."

Chapter Thirteen

"Gather the village for their new king's wedding!" Haakon boomed as they re-entered the fort. He held up his hands. "We will feast and celebrate, then when the sun sets I will bed my beautiful bride."

"You are a king now?" Noah said with a sideways glance.

"It is my destiny to rule." Haakon banged his chest and grinned. He carried on walking at speed. "Which makes me a king."

Kenna spotted her mother coming from the well with a bucket. "Mother." She rushed to her and took the water. "He has done it. He has become Christian in order to marry me."

"Lord, give us strength." Her mother shook her head. "And give *you* strength, for I have just heard him holler to the entire village that he intends to bed you later."

Kenna shivered at the thought. "And, Mother..." She didn't know how to form the sentence.

"What?" Her mother squeezed Kenna's arm as they walked. "Tell me."

"He... He has..."

"What?"

"Oh, it is so sinful. He has a metal ring, down there, through the end of his..."

"No!"

"Aye, apparently, it was a gift from his mother, to ensure a woman's pleasure."

Her mother crossed herself. "What kind of woman was his mother? That is indeed a sin."

"And I have to…" Kenna swallowed. "Take that inside myself. I will burst, surely, it is so big. *He* is so big."

"And unlikely to be gentle. Men like him do not know their own strength."

Kenna's eyes misted and her chest squeezed. "I will have to pray to God that it is quick."

"Kenna, my love!" Haakon boomed in her direction. "We will wed at midday." He pointed to the sun that was peeking through the sludgy, gray clouds. "Ensure you are ready for me."

"He is very determined," Hamish said, coming alongside Kenna and their mother. "I will give him that." He paused. "And he has angered his fiery sister. That is not something I envy him of."

"Aye, he has and she is a demon," Kenna said. "But I have other concerns. Concerns for myself."

"I will be close at all times, sister, and I will lay down my life to protect you should he hurt you." Hamish set his hand on her shoulder.

"I thank you, Hamish. You are kind and dear to me." She sighed. "But this is a cross a woman must bear alone." She watched Haakon stride toward the Great House. His paces were long and a damp patch had spread on the back of his tunic where his hair had dripped. He didn't appear to notice trivial things like the icy temperature of the day.

"They have been working all morning, the Vikings." Bryce appeared, hand on his dagger. "Building and banging and converting the Great House for their own use. They have taken over." He spat on the ground.

"It is preferable to them killing us all." Noah looked at Olaf.

"I agree." Olaf tugged his long beard, smoothing the tip into a point. "Which is what I believed they would do when I first saw them. We should send our thanks to God that we are standing here breathing, talking, that we have blood in our veins and so do our loved ones."

"It's all well and good for you to say that." Kenna gestured at Olaf. "*You* don't have to be bedded by him."

"My child." Olaf pressed his palms to her cheeks. "God will give you strength in your moment of need."

"I'd prefer some strong ale." She clicked her tongue on the roof of her mouth.

"Come, Kenna," her mother said. "We must get you ready for your new husband. We do not wish to anger him."

"What I should do is run for the mountains." Kenna glanced to her right and saw their peaks rising into the clouds. "He doesn't know this land; he wouldn't find me there."

"I think he would." Hamish shook his head. "He has abandoned the gods he grew up with, his people's gods, in order to have you. He barely thought twice about it. I don't think there is anything he wouldn't do to have you. To make you his and have you by his side."

"Thanks for that!" Kenna glared at him. "How to make me feel really fucking trapped."

"You are not trapped." Her mother wrapped her arm around Kenna's waist. "You are saving your village. You are following God's rich path, the one He has set out for you."

"Like a martyr," Kenna huffed. "Oh, good. How lucky I am."

FOUR HOURS LATER, when the sun had left the sky and a chill had seeped into the air, Kenna sat at a table in the renovated Great House beside her giant of a new husband. A harpist played in the corner, but its melodic sound was drowned out by the din of the festivities.

"*Skál! Skál!*" Haakon shouted for the tenth time as he held up his mug of ale. "How lucky a man am I." He laughed and drank and his fellow Vikings did the same.

"Congratulations to King Rory," Hamish said loudly.

Haakon stilled and stared at him. "I am King Haakon."

"You have a new Christian name."

"That I do not wish to use...yet." Haakon spun his finger in the air. "So many changes to get used to. I will take them one at a time. Or maybe two at a time. For right now, I am getting used to being both king and a husband."

Hamish looked about to argue but then thought better of it.

"Eat, my brother by law," Haakon said, gesturing to the food. "Eat and be merry with me."

A feast of pork, fish, bone broth, honeyed porridge, and fresh bread had been laid on. Sweet heather ale flowed and squat candles burned brightly in every corner and on every table. But while Haakon and his friends acted as if all were right in the world, like they were having the time of their lives, the villagers were subdued and wary. They threw furtive glances at their new king and his men—always on edge, clearly waiting for permission to leave the marital festivities and retreat to their small homes.

"The Bible says all sorrows will pass," Kenna said, leaning closer to Hamish.

"That, I will pray for." Hamish paused. "I haven't seen the sister, not since the beach."

"No, neither have I." Kenna glanced around the room. Gunnar was sloshing ale into his mug. "She is indeed very angry with her brother."

"As you would be with me if I turned my back on God. Which I would never do."

"I know you wouldn't." She paused. "Maybe you should go and look for Haakon's sister, Hamish."

"What? Why? Why me?" He shrugged then glanced around.

"She seems to like you, and if I have to wed a heathen, then why shouldn't you?"

Hamish frowned. "She does not like me—she looks at me with disdain. Clearly, she sees me as an inferior race. There is no way on this Earth I would marry her."

Kenna shrugged. She couldn't entirely dismiss his point. Astrid did give glares that could wither a fresh flower.

"*Skál*, oh, beautiful wife of mine." Haakon leaned close to her, his arm brushing hers and his body heat seeming to wrap around her. "I am indeed a lucky man. The envy of every man in this room and more should they see you."

His gaze drifted down her body, hovering at the neckline of her yellow, woolen gown and the fish-shaped brooch that fastened the material in place. He slid his tongue over his bottom lip and nodded slowly. "*Ja*, very lucky, indeed."

Her belly tightened and she twisted a loop of hair around her finger, fidgeting on the chair.

"Do not fear," he said with a grin. "Soon, the celebrations will come to an end and I will take you into the new bedchamber I have had made just for us. It is a place where our passion and desire for each other will know no bounds."

"You mean *your* passion and desire." She reached for her drink. "For I have none. I will merely tolerate yours."

He frowned and slammed down his mug. Ale splashed onto his hand. "You speak like a belligerent wife."

"Maybe I am." She held his eye contact. "For it was *you* who wished to marry me. I never once wished to marry you."

He leaned closer. "You said the vows before your God. You betrothed yourself to me until death do us part."

"'Haps I wish for that death to come quickly."

"No." He curled his hand around the back of her neck, his fingers tight, and drew her face closer to his. "Do not speak of your death, for that would break me into a thousand pieces. I could not breathe without you, not now I know you."

She stared into his eyes. They brimmed with emotion and sparkled with sincerity. Her heart rate picked up and her mind filled with thoughts. The rest of the room seemed to fade away. He truly meant his words, she could see that. "But...why?" she whispered. "You have just met me. How can you feel so strongly?"

He kept a tight hold of her and a muscle flexed in his cheek. "Because you are my destiny. You saved my life, and now you will complete my life. I will slay any man or woman or animal that hurts you. I will spend the rest of my days, until my last breath, making you happy, giving you everything I can provide, making you the mother of our children and swearing to protect them with everything I am."

She tried to duck her chin to break his intense eye contact, but he kept her looking up at him. "But... But you don't know me, or this land, or—"

"I know enough to know I want all the knowledge, of everything. It is true I am a great warrior and a fine seafarer, but I am also a farmer, a fisherman, and now a husband." His mouth stretched into a gentle smile. "So believe my words, because one thing I am not is a liar."

Her mouth was suddenly dry and her breaths shallow. "But your kind, they—"

"Do not judge me on the actions of others. Judge me on my own actions." He released her and sat back, scooping up his drink again. "That is all I ask of you."

Kenna was quiet as she looked down at the bread and pork on her plate. She had no appetite, yet her mother had told her to eat well, for she'd need her strength on her wedding night.

With a shaking hand, she picked up the bread and tore off the crust, chewing on it.

"Listen to me, your king." Haakon suddenly stood, knocking the table with his fist. "For I wish to speak to you, my good people."

Kenna caught her drink before it toppled.

The room went quiet.

"My wife and I," Haakon said, candlelight flickering over his face, "are thankful that you feast with us on our wedding day, and I thank you for providing that feast. We"—he gestured to Gunnar, Knud, Orm, Egil, and Ivar, who were chewing noisily and reaching for more food—"are new to this land, but I promise from this day on, we will pull our weight and work the pastures and sea with you. We will learn from you, we will summer and winter with you, and should enemy arrive on our threshold, we will fight with you." He held his drink aloft. "Give my wife a good cheer to celebrate her beauty."

A small ripple of cheer went around the room, eyes were wide, and cheeks a little flushed from the warmth of the fire troughs.

"Come on!" Haakon set his hand on Kenna's head. "More than that. She is a goddess."

Kenna wasn't used to having such praise. Part of her liked it, but the part of her that had always fought to be as good as her brother and Bryce bristled. She was more than a face and hair and breasts. She was skilled and admired for her survival skills.

The cheer was louder this time. Loud enough for Haakon to apparently be satisfied. He set back his shoulders and grinned. "And now… Now you can all take the last of your plates and leave, for I wish to be alone with my bride." He looked down at her. "For I am a lucky man and my cock wishes to receive its prize of a tight cunny."

"Oh, help us, Lord." Kenna's mother fanned herself. "What a thing to say."

Orm laughed and slapped his thighs. "Oh, indeed, you are a fortunate heathen, Haakon. For that is what you are. Dipping into the sea has not changed the way the Great Hall of gods look upon you."

"It has changed everything." Haakon frowned at him. "And you too, go. I wish for this building to be empty on this night. Find somewhere else to sleep. All of you." He flicked his hand at his brother and friends.

The village people didn't need telling twice and in a scrape of chair legs and a fluster of cloaks and furs, they stood and scrambled for the door.

"Where will we go?" Gunnar asked, wiping the back of his hand on his mouth.

"I don't care. The cave, if necessary."

Orm stood. "We will find Astrid. She must have discovered an empty dwelling."

"Astrid." Haakon looked around. "She is not here?"

"I believe you have angered her." Kenna looked up at him.

"Why?" He frowned.

"For becoming Christian."

"She'll have to get used to it." He stooped and wrapped his arm around her waist, pulling her to standing. "Because it is not changing now. My path is set on the same one as yours."

His muscles were so hard and unyielding. His body hot and solid. She stiffened against him, unused to having her personal space invaded by a huge man who touched her with such ownership.

"Go!" he ordered the room again, his voice deep and firm. "We wish to be alone."

A tremble attacked Kenna, spreading down her spine to her arms and legs. She clamped her thighs together and her breasts felt heavy. Soon, he'd claim her and there was nothing she could do to stop it.

His brother and friends stood, their height dwarfing the last of the villagers as they made their way to the door. When they'd left she spotted Hamish looking at her from the shadows. A line had formed between his eyes and he was gnawing on his cheek.

"*Go,*" she mouthed. For what could her brother do now?

He hesitated then with stiff shoulders turned and left.

"My bride," Haakon said. "This is my gift for you."

He steered her from the table toward a thick, dark blanket that had been used as a door into a newly formed room. "I hope you will like it."

As he pulled it back, she saw that the Great House had indeed been transformed. Now the entire curved back wall was paneled and set in the center of it was a huge, dark-framed bed covered in furs and feather pillows. Shelves held candles and an iron basket hung from the roof, scarlet embers glowing within it. The floor was heavy with overlapping rugs and a round table held a jug and goblets as well as a basket of bannock rolls.

"What do you think?" he asked, his hand pressing on the small of her back and urging her inside.

She looked at the stag antlers set upon the wall and then the cross next to it.

"My men worked hard, as did your village carpenter, Hywel."

"I can see that."

"He is an excellent craftsman."

"That is something I know."

He stepped into the room, letting the rug fall behind him, closing them off from the main hall. "And the bed is large enough for three or four people should we wish to invite other lovers to join us."

Her mouth fell open in shock. "'Other lovers'?"

"I am not opposed to women joining us. Two or three, should the urge take us."

"'Other women'?" She held up her hands. "I… What? I mean…"

"Ah, I see you do not wish to share me." He chuckled and tapped her chin with his finger. "I cannot say that I am upset by your jealousy. In fact, it pleases me."

"*Jealousy.* You cannot be serious." She gestured to the bed. "In fact, I would rather you choose another to lie with you."

He hesitated, his lips a tight line, then he pulled off his tunic and tossed it onto a chair in the corner. "You should also strip."

"Strip?"

"*Ja*, remove your gown. I wish to see exactly what has come into my possession."

And a possession was what she felt like. She was his. There was no way of getting out of that now. In the eyes of God, they were man and wife and she'd have to do her duty.

Chapter Fourteen

Haakon shoved at his pants, then huffed and had to sit and remove his boots too. When he was fully naked he stood, hands on hips, and watched his new wife slowly unpeel from her gown.

His cock stiffened. Oh, she was a beauty. Her breasts were round and ripe, her nipples pink and tight. Her waist was small and the flare of her hips told him she'd be fertile and strong. And her skin, it was the shade of milk and as delicate as a feather. He licked his lips; the urge to kiss her all over and learn her taste and shape was almost overwhelming.

She turned and set her folded gown on the end of the bed.

His throat tightened when he saw her apple-round ass for the first time. He clenched his fists, imagining palming its softness as he sank deep into her pussy.

"What do you want me to do?" she said in a stiff, little voice.

"Lie on the bed." His stomach clenched and his balls tingled. He took his cock in his hand and fingered the ring at the end, enjoying how it heightened his arousal.

She did as he'd asked and he savored the moment of watching her move. Outside, the wind had picked up, rattling something nearby—*clang, clang*—but he barely noticed. She had his entire attention.

The hair at the juncture of her thighs was dark and untrimmed and her legs were long and elegant, the muscles defined as she moved. Likely, she could run well, swim too. That thought pleased him.

She lay back on the furs with her hands curled into fists and her eyes screwed up tight.

"There is no need to look as though you are about to be sacrificed against your will to appease the gods," he said, stepping up to the bed.

"'Haps that is how I feel." She kept her eyes closed.

"I will bring you pleasure." His cock was at full hardness, solid in his hand, and the tip tingled with anticipation of pushing into her wetness. "Don't you believe me?"

"'Pleasure.'" She grimaced. "I can't imagine that for a moment. Pain. Mortification. Disgust. That is what I expect."

He froze and his heart turned leaden. "What did you just say?"

"You heard me." She opened her eyes and glared at his face. It seemed as though she were avoiding looking at his cock, which was odd. Most women openly salivated for him.

"I heard *disgust* and *pain*, which hurts me here." He banged his chest with his free hand as the breath squeezed in his lungs. "And it not what a woman should say to a man on their wedding night."

"Oh, just get on with it, will you?"

She opened her legs a fraction and a tremble went over her gooseflesh skin, her breasts shaking slightly.

An urge to take her in his arms, hold her, kiss her, show her that his body would only bring hers pleasure gripped him, but he held back.

"Please, be quick." She reached for the cross that sat in the hollow of her throat and kissed it. "God be with me."

"God be with you?" He released his cock. "Why would you say that now, of all nights?"

"Because you are a big man. This will hurt."

"I have no intention of causing you pain, but if you do not relax…" He sat on the bed and brushed his thumb over her nipple. "Then—"

His words were cut short when she flinched away from him. Suddenly, his entire body felt unbearably heavy with disappointment. She really didn't want him. Really didn't see him as the virile Viking he was.

Disgust.

That was what she'd said.

His cock deflated and he sighed loudly.

"Please, just do it. I won't fight you and I won't scream." She pursed her lips so tight, they went almost white. "But I beg you to be quick."

"No!"

"No?" She opened her eyes. "But...?"

He stood and walked away from her, grabbing his pants. "I am a man and a lover. Women want me, *beg* for me, and I will not take you—even if you are my wife—if you do not want me to."

She sat, elbows locked behind her. "But you...you said...?"

"I know what I said and I know what I want: to fuck you. But I am not someone who finds pleasure when my partner does not." He shoved his legs into his pants then hopped on the spot as he pulled them up and tied the waist. "So hear this, Kenna: you will remain unsatisfied until you are begging for me, begging for my cock. Until you feel remorse for calling me 'disgusting,' until you feel like you will die if I do not fuck you all day and all night. Until then, you will not have me." He tipped his chin. "I bid you goodnight."

He flicked the rug and left the room he'd been so excited to show her. A part of him wanted to storm back in, shuck his pants, and take her hard and fast. Show her what she was missing. Prove to her they could be so good together. That his pierced cock could give her pleasure she didn't even know existed.

But he didn't. Instead, he poured ale, drank deep, then sat and stared at the door, which was rattling in the wind. For the first time, he wondered if he'd made a mistake leaving Drangar. These people were tolerating him. He'd scared them into allowing him to stay. Was that really what he wanted? Was that really how to make himself belong?

And he'd demanded Kenna marry him. But wasn't that his right? To choose a wife? He could have had any woman he'd chosen back in Drangar. They'd all wanted him and his big cock and his title.

But here...?

Kenna.

She'd gritted her teeth and prayed to her god to take her away from the bed in which he wished to love her.

Fuck it.

What was he going to do?

How could he get her to desire him the way he desired her?

He'd dunked himself into the bitterly cold ocean and walked away from the gods he'd revered all of his life for her. Spared an entire village...for her. What more could she expect of him?

AT SOME POINT, Haakon felt his eyes grow heavy, and knowing Kenna was safely in their new marital bed, he allowed sleep to come over him. The room was warm—though outside, a storm blew—and his belly was full.

When he woke, daylight sliced beneath the door along with a small drift of snow. The cockerel crowed and in the distance, the farrier banged and the carpenter sawed.

He'd slept for hours. With a stiff spine, he sat forward and ran his hand through his hair. Glancing at the blanket partition, he saw it had been disturbed.

Quickly, he got up and looked into the bedchamber. Kenna was gone.

"How did she...?" He snatched up his boots. Haakon prided himself in sleeping light and noticing anything that went on around him. Yet his new bride had managed to sneak past him like a tiny dormouse.

He made a growling sound and finished dressing, then he stormed from the Great House, ignoring the tables still holding the remnants of the feast.

"Where is she?" he hollered at Hamish.

Hamish looked up from where he was hammering a fence around the snow-laden chicken coop.

"I don't know."

"Don't lie to me." Haakon marched up to him.

"I really don't know." Hamish shrugged. "I'm not lying."

The nonchalant manner made Haakon want to thump him, but he resisted. Hitting his new wife's brother, likely knocking out a few teeth, wouldn't get him into her good books.

"You must have an idea," he snarled.

"She sets traps, down by the river. Likely, she has gone to check on them."

"She goes out alone? And you let her? A woman from these lands?"

"She is a determined woman with many skills honed in these forests." Hamish's jaw tightened. "And likely, she wanted to clear her head after a night with you."

Haakon balled his fists. "And where is my sister?"

"It is not my job to keep track of everyone in the village." Hamish turned and banged a nail with his hammer, sending snow skittering from the wooden fence.

Haakon scowled at Hamish's broad back then checked his dagger was on his belt. It was. There was only one thing for it. He'd have to find his wife himself.

Striding past Kenna's family home, he spotted Noah. "Is your daughter in there?"

Noah looked up from feeding pigs. "No. We thought she was with you."

Haakon gritted his teeth and made for the exit of the fort. He strode through it, his feet dipping into a layer of freshly fallen snow.

Beyond the watchtower, a few villagers tended animals and another chopped logs. He marched past them, caring for no one except Kenna.

And then he saw them, small footprints heading west toward the forest. They could only be hers, surely.

Breaking into a run, he followed them, his breath puffing in front of his face and his legs pounding.

He noticed dark clouds to the north. Likely, Thor was angry with him for being baptized. Would they all suffer his thunderous wrath or would it just be him? He ducked into the forest, still following the footprints. Tree branches were heavy with snow and a stiff breeze stirred flakes into the air. He spotted animal tracks—rabbit, squirrel, deer—and birds flitted from branch to branch.

A raven cawed up ahead and he paused, knowing that not only was Thor on the horizon, but Odin was also watching him.

"I am sorry, All Father," he said, pushing on. He wanted to say more but didn't know how to explain his need for Kenna superseded everything else.

Where was she?

Suddenly, he stopped. His blood ran as cold as the river running alongside him.

In the distance, a wolf howled, no doubt lamenting the lack of food this time of year. Its stomach would be rumbling, forcing it to be brave and reckless.

"Kenna!" He broke into a run, following Kenna's tracks and also searching frantically for wolf prints. Were they stalking her?

He'd kill every damn one of them if they were.

As Haakon turned alongside a meander in the river, the footprints changed. They were scuffed and haphazard.

Quickly, he stopped and spotted a trap. It had been reset. Recently, he'd guess.

She'd been here. And not long ago.

Another wolf howl made the hairs on the back of his neck stand on end.

He sprinted forward.

At his side, the river narrowed and deepened, another tributary adding to it. The water was ice blue as it crashed over menacing, hard rocks, rushing down from the mountain and frothing and crashing as it went.

The footprints ran alongside the river and were fresh. He had to have been gaining on her.

And then he saw her standing dead still, red-feathered arrow at the ready in a small bow.

He came to a halt, breathing hard and with his heart racing.

He held his breath as he spotted the pheasant she had in her aim.

What a beauty she was, and a huntress too. Everything about her intrigued him.

Suddenly, the pheasant was startled by a jumping squirrel, sending snow tumbling downward onto it.

She fired her arrow, anyway, and was still as close as he'd have been under the circumstances.

"Kenna!"

She turned, eyes wide and cheeks flushed. "Get away from me!"

"We should speak."

"No!" She stepped to the right, toward the river, then down the bank to its gushing fury. She went out of view.

"Fuck! Wait!" he called, rushing to where she'd disappeared. "Please. Let's talk." Fear gripped him. He knew the power of water and he also knew the determination of an angry woman.

Combined…anything could happen.

Chapter Fifteen

Kenna half-slid and half-slipped down the icy bank. She had no intention of going back to the village. She'd catch some food and make herself at home in a cave until Haakon gave up on her and went back to whatever hellhole he'd come from.

With her bow slotted over her shoulder, she glanced right and left and held up her gown so she could see her boots. The stepping stones were just visible above the freezing water. If she could get to the other side, she'd be able to run along the bank and hopefully lose her tracks in driftwood debris.

Because that was how he'd found her, and it proved what an addled state her mind was in that she hadn't thought to cover them.

"Kenna!"

She couldn't see him, but she could hear him.

Tentatively, she stepped onto the first stone. It was slippery underfoot, but she had good balance and reached for the next, arms outstretched to steady herself. Her ears filled with the sound of the water racing around her, competing with the tempo of her racing heart.

As she'd lain fractious in bed all night, feeling sure he'd come and claim her in the most brutal of ways, a plan to escape had formed.

It wasn't a good plan, or one that went far into the future, but perhaps if she could escape for a few days, she'd come up with a better one. Maybe travel east and join another community, pretend the marriage had never happened. After all, it hadn't been consummated, so in the eyes of God, the deal had yet to be sealed.

She sensed a shadow at her side and looked up.

He was there on the bank. Big and looming. His eyes wide and his nostrils flaring. "Kenna, the water is too fast. It will take your feet."

"Leave me alone." Urgency gripped her and she leaped to the next stone, wobbled for a second, then regained her balance.

The river was deep here, too deep to see the bottom or even guess where it was. A branch whizzed past her, bashing against a rock, spinning around then disappearing downstream.

"Be careful!" he yelled over the noise.

"Leave me alone." She eyed the next stone. It was farther away than the last.

"Kenna! No!" The wind buffeted his shout. "Don't do it. I beg you."

A rush of determination gripped her and she leaped into the air, the bow bouncing on her back.

But no amount of determination could land her safely. The stone was suddenly deluged with a torrent of water, disappearing completely, and when her toe did hit it, the mossy surface meant there was no chance of grip.

The next thing she knew, she was flailing in the air and looking up at the angry sky. When the cold mountain water wrapped around her, it bellowed into her ears, rushed up her nose, and spiked her with a thousand daggers of ice.

And then she was rushing downstream like the branch had done. Battling for air, she pushed to the surface and grabbed a lung full.

She'd survive—she could swim. She just had to…

The water spun her around. It was disorientating, breath-snatching and freezing. The inside of her nose stung and the ball of her ankle hit a rock, pain lashing up her leg. Her gown tangled around her limbs, making it harder to swim—if she was swimming at all, that was. It was more like being stolen away.

Again, she struck out, hoping to find something to cling to. But it was just rushing water all around—fast, violent, malicious.

"Kenna! Grab my hand."

She spun downstream and spotted Haakon. He'd anchored himself to a fallen tree and was holding out his arm at full stretch and half-hanging over the rushing water.

"Grab it!" he yelled. "I will save you."

She swallowed a mouthful of water, spluttered, and tried to angle herself toward him. The river widened over a steep fall soon; she had to get out before she hit that. She wouldn't survive the drop.

Haakon's hand was suddenly a beacon of hope.

If only she could grab it.

In a sudden rush, his outstretched fingers were above her. *He* was above her. She reached out desperately. Their fingers brushed for a split second, then she felt a firm grip around her forearm and she was being pulled.

It was as if a giant had reached for her. She shot upward, the water falling away and her clothes clinging to her body. On and up, she went. The fallen tree creaked and then strong, pincer-like arms were around her torso.

"You're safe. I've got you," Haakon said into her ear, his breath hot on her icy skin.

She was breathing hard and fast; her heart beat so wildly, she felt it would fly from her chest. But she was alive. She was out of the water.

Her new husband had saved her.

"Get off me," she said, pushing at him. But her strength had gone. She had no fight left in her.

Haakon ignored her feeble wriggling and scooted with surprising agility back along the tree trunk and set her, and himself, on the snowy bank.

She pushed her wet hair from her face as a full-body shiver attacked her.

"Are you hurt?" he asked, cupping her cheeks and staring into her eyes.

Her ankle throbbed and the cold was like a thousand midge bites. "I'm fine."

"You could have been killed." He frowned and shook his head. "What in Thor's name were you thinking?"

"I was thinking that I've married a heathen, something you've just proven."

"What?"

"In *Thor's* name. That is what you said."

He paused. "I meant in *God's* name, what were you thinking?"

"That I had to escape. Get away."

"From me?"

"Aye." She turned and hitched her gown above her ankles. Her bow and arrows were long gone.

"But I didn't hurt you. I didn't come to you much, as I wanted you. I let you rest last night and—"

"Ouch!" Her ankle gave way, the one that had bashed up against the stone. Pain sliced through delicate flesh and bone.

Instantly, he was there, his arms around her again. "What is it? Where are you hurt?"

"Nowhere... I..." She dragged up the sodden material and saw that her boot had been torn by the sharp rock and a bloody cut gauged through her flesh. "That stupid rock." She huffed. How the heck was she going to walk home now? It felt like it had been twisted around on a millstone.

"You are hurt," he said, "and freezing cold too."

"I... I'm not too cold." She shivered violently.

He made a frustrated, grunting sound then stooped and took her into his arms. He swung her upward and against his chest.

"What are you doing? Put me down."

"You can't walk and you'll freeze to death if we don't get you back to Tillicoulty soon."

"I can walk."

"You can walk as well as I can recite that God book of yours…"

"The Bible."

"*Ja*. The Bible."

She frowned and studied the determined look on his face as he strode along the snowy riverbank, retracing the way they'd come.

"And if the wolves smell blood," he said, glancing around, "that won't be good, either."

"The wolves stay higher in the mountains."

"Not the one I heard—it was close. Too close for comfort when there's an injury."

It was as if she weighed nothing at all. Haakon took ground-eating paces, holding her tightly, his breath huffing in front of him.

She looped her arms around his neck, glad of the warmth of his body, though it did little to help with the shivers that were rattling up her spine. Had she ever been so cold? So chilled to the bone? She didn't think so and the damn northern wind wasn't helping at all.

"You nearly got that pheasant," he said gruffly. "You are a good huntress."

"My father… taught me and Hamish… when we were young. I have had many years… practicing." Her jaw was practically frozen in place.

"And your trap was a good design. I was surprised you caught nothing."

He was complimenting her skills? She hadn't expected that from him. Wasn't he only interested in bedding her and planting his seed? Taking what he could from the village and the villagers? "It is a lean month… for meat. Though I did get a boarlet… a few days… ago."

He raised his eyebrows and ducked back onto the forest track. "This time of year?"

"A late brood. Foolish of the… mother."

"I agree." He paused. "But it is good to know there is meat to hunt here all year round."

She was quiet. He really had gotten his feet under the table. He wasn't going anywhere.

Suddenly, he stopped and his breath hitched.

"What?" With her teeth chattering violently, she looked in the direction he was.

Her heart skipped a beat and panic soared through her body. Fight or flight.

Staring at them was a sandy-furred wolf. Drool dripped from its bared fangs and its blue eyes were set on them. With its ears pricked forward and hackles spiked upward, it appeared intent on attack, brave with it.

"I told you it was close," Haakon said, glancing around. "But I can't see any others."

The creature let out a low growl and a threatening snap of its sharp teeth. It then took a step forward, its big pads digging deep into the snow.

Kenna grabbed at her waist with numb fingers. "I… I haven't got my dagger." It must have fallen off her belt in the water.

"I have mine." Slowly, he set her down. "Can you stand for a moment?"

"Aye…but…" She adjusted her weight onto her good leg and gripped a lichen-covered tree trunk. "What are you…going to…?"

"It's not a problem. I will get rid of him."

"He's hungry…and dangerous." She cursed her chattering teeth. They were out of control.

"Not as dangerous as me." He winked at her, gave the cockiest grin she'd ever seen a man give, then took out his dagger and raised it above his head.

Then with a roar she didn't think a human could make, he raced forward, charging at the wolf with his furred cloak flapping and his feet thumping through the snow, kicking it up this way and that.

For a moment, the wolf just stared at him. Confusion seemed to flash through its glacial eyes. Then it sprang into action, lunging forward at Haakon.

Haakon flapped his arms, roaring louder, and the weak sunlight glinted off the dagger.

The wolf, seeming now to be a fraction of Haakon's size, suddenly had a loss of courage and its tail slunk between its legs and it shifted to the side. For a heartbeat, it stilled, head lowered, then it turned and took off into the shadows of a fir tree.

"*Ja*, that's it. Be gone. Be gone, wolf. There is nothing here for you!" Haakon yelled, shaking the tree branches and creating a small snowstorm.

"He's gone?" Kenna asked, peering into the darkness.

"*Ja*, and he won't be back. He knows I'll kill him." Haakon was at her side, his dagger once again on his belt. "My love, you are so pale."

"I'm…I'm cold." She could barely think of anything else. Her fingers, toes, and limbs were numb and her belly a tight knot of ice.

"Here, wear this." He took off his fur and threw it around her shoulders.

Instantly, the warmth of it penetrated her skin. For a moment, she closed her eyes.

"We need to get you warmed up back at the village." He swung her into his arms. "It will not take long, my beautiful wife. I will get you there."

Kenna closed her eyes, lost to everything except the pain in her ankle and the cold that seemed to pierce into her very soul.

Haakon rushed through the forest with her tight in his arms. She didn't like that she felt so helpless. In fact, she hated it. But what choice did she have? She was freezing to death and couldn't walk. If he hadn't plucked her from the raging torrent of water, she'd be dead by now. In the name of the Lord, if he hadn't been carrying her back to the village, she'd have been dead too.

A spark of hot anger gripped her. If Haakon hadn't chased her and forced her to cross the river using the stepping stones, she wouldn't have been in this position at all. She could have been in a little cave with a fire, alone, forming an escape plan.

She balled her fists and clutched his fur tighter. The sounds of the village were approaching and she wasn't sure how they'd gotten there so quickly. A dog barked—Lass, she thought—and someone was chopping logs.

"We are here," he said. "Soon, I will warm you and all will be well."

"What has happened to her?" A woman's voice.

Kenna cracked open her eyes. Astrid was pacing beside them. Dagger on her belt and her hair flicking in the wind.

"She fell into the river, and her ankle is cut." Haakon kept pacing.

"Her lips are blue—that's not good."

"It would have been less good if she'd gone over the fall. I could hear it. She was moments away."

"The waterfall goddess, Saga, nearly took her?" Astrid exclaimed. "She is always hungry for the weak."

"Kenna is not weak." Haakon growled. "She fought hard. That is why she is here."

Astrid huffed.

"She is also an accomplished hunter and trapper."

"I'll believe that when I see it."

Haakon scowled. "Be of help, will you? Run ahead and stoke the fire in our bedchamber."

"Can't your new god do it for you? Seems to me he's all-powerful."

"Astrid. We haven't got time to argue."

She sighed, muttered something in a language Kenna didn't understand, then disappeared.

"We are here now. Soon, you will be warm." Haakon strode under the watchtower.

"Kenna! Oh, what is wrong with her?"

"Mother?" Kenna said, but she felt too weak to open her eyes.

"She fell into the river. She is cold, but I will warm her up."

"And her leg? Is that blood?"

"It is a clean gash. I will bandage it."

"No, I will do it. Bring her to our home."

"She lives with me now and the fire is being stoked in preparation for her."

"But... Mother. I want my mother." Kenna tried to reach out, but her cold arms wouldn't work.

"I can and will care for her," Haakon said firmly. "And if I do not do that to Kenna's approval, I will walk away from Tillicoulty."

"You'll what?" Noah said.

"You heard." Haakon huffed. "And I am a man of my word. If Kenna says that I have not cared for her, my men and I will leave your village and never return."

"And if she dies?" Noah asked.

"She will not. I will not let her."

Kenna whimpered and was aware of the light changing. They were inside the Great House now. The scent of the feast and sweet ale still hung in the air. And the air was warmer. Fire troughs were glowing.

"Do not fear. Your ordeal is almost over," Haakon said.

Kenna found herself being laid on the soft bed. She shivered and tried to move her bitterly cold limbs. They weren't working.

She could hear the fire crackling, logs being stacked. Smoke and ash tickled her nose.

"This needs to come off," Haakon said, pulling at her gown.

"Okay, but...I can do it." She tried to sit but couldn't. "Oh..."

"Your blood has all but frozen to ice in your veins," Haakon said. "This wet gown needs to come off before you can get warm."

He was peeling it over her head, exposing her nakedness beneath.

"How you thought you'd survive with so little clothing on..." he muttered.

"The fire is lit," Astrid said.

Kenna cracked open her eyes. Astrid was standing at the end of the bed, hands on her hips, frowning at Kenna's naked form.

"Good," Haakon said, shucking off his tunic. "Go and warm broth."

"Huh, I'll tell her mother to do it."

"No." Haakon stooped and pulled at his boots. "I've told them I will care for her. I need to prove that I can, that I always will."

"This nonsense will have angered all the gods," Astrid said, shaking out the gown then hanging it on a hook. "You will get what is coming to you."

"And I will take it. Remember the runes? I am following the path I was shown."

Astrid frowned and folded her arms.

"Please. Broth," Haakon said, shoving at his pants so that he too was naked.

"What? No, please," Kenna managed. "Not now?" Not when her trembling was uncontrollable and she couldn't feel her hands and feet? Surely not. Surely, he wouldn't take her now.

"Oh, in the name of the gods," Astrid snapped. "I'll get the broth."

She left the room.

Kenna crossed her arms over her naked breasts. Her nipples were tight and chilled. "Please, I...I need..."

"You need body heat," Haakon said, climbing onto the bed and shifting furs around. "It is the only way to warm you. The quickest way to warm you."

Kenna gasped as he pulled her close, wrapping her in his big, hot arms, settling her against his chest, then coiling his legs with hers as though trying to touch as much of her as he could at once.

A fur settled over them, then another as he dragged the soft material upward.

"Oh!" she said, the longed-for heat finally touching her skin. "Aye...oh...that's better." She closed her eyes, knowing that the cock resting against her hip would get hard, would then be demanding of her.

"Shh." He kissed the top of her head and smoothed her tangled hair. "Rest now. Soon, my heat will be shared with you and you will stop shivering."

As he spoke the word 'shivering,' a particularly violent tremble went up her spine and over her scalp.

"It's not a problem," he said softly. "Nothing is going to happen except you are going to get warm. You will be well. I promise."

"My ankle." It was throbbing with more intensity now. "It...hurts."

"When you are warm and the danger is over, we will examine it properly. Astrid bandaged it."

"She did?"

"*Ja.*"

Kenna realized she must have been numb with cold, for she hadn't felt a thing.

"But try not to sleep," Haakon said. "Stay awake. It will be better."

"Better?"

"For then I will not fear you have been taken to another realm before my heat could revive you."

"Another realm? Don't you mean...heaven?"

"*Ja*, that is what I mean. Your heaven. *Our* heaven."

"You have a lot to learn."

"I am not afraid of that." Again, he smoothed her hair. It was a gentle caress that calmed her heart rate.

She could feel his heartbeat too, and his breaths blowing warm on her head. If he was true to his word and this was about putting life back into her body, perhaps being naked in bed with him wasn't so bad, after all.

Chapter Sixteen

"Tell me…" Kenna murmured against the base of Haakon's neck. Her eyes felt heavy and she feared a deep and dreamless sleep she would not wake up from was encroaching. "About your gods."

"You want a saga?" he asked quietly.

"If you have one."

"I have many. What would you like to hear about?"

She paused. "A love story."

"A love story." He chuckled, his chest shifting against hers, and his body hair catching on her nipples. "I will think of one."

He was quiet for a moment, then, "I will tell you of Freya, the Goddess of War."

"A goddess of war?"

"*Ja*, she is a fine warrior viqueen with a chariot drawn by beautiful, strong, wild cats. She liked to race her brother, always determined to beat him." He paused and kind of huffed. "As determined as her father, Njord, the God of the Sea, was that day he tipped us into the water and smashed up our boat."

Kenna was quiet, imagining a wild, Viking woman, a viqueen, racing along in a chariot pulled by wild cats. It was quite the image.

Haakon ran his hand up her back as though checking her skin for returning heat. She pressed against him, needing all the warmth she could get.

"On Earth, in our realm," Haakon went on. "A man lived, called

'Otta.' He was a simple man, with farmland, and worshipped Freya so much, he built a delicate and detailed stone shrine to make many offerings to her. Freya adored Otta because he was devoted to her, loved her, and so she looked down upon him often." He paused. "Are you still awake?"

She nodded.

"Good." He ran his hand to the small of her back and pressed her closer, his legs tightening in their twist with hers.

Kenna wriggled her fingers and toes. Life was returning to them.

"But one day, Otta found himself in trouble. His land was under threat. Others wanted to take it from him. He had no heirs and no recollection of his mother and father or any of his ancestors. So Freya came down to Earth and promised to help him, as he was such a pious follower. Otta was of course delighted to meet his goddess and even when she told him she must disguise him as a boar, he agreed."

"Why did he have to be disguised?"

"Because she was taking him to another realm, Asgard, and he was not dead. For Freya is the Goddess of War and with that, she is the ruler of the Valkyrie and their job is to take the fallen to Valhalla." He kissed the top of her head again, his lips lingering. "The Valkyrie are very beautiful, very strong and wise, just like you."

She lifted her head and looked up at him.

His eyes were a softer blue than she'd seen them before and the frown line between them had gone.

"What happened when they got to Asgard?" Kenna asked, becoming very aware of his hands gently smoothing over her skin.

"Ah, that is where the story is interesting. They came across a cave, the home of a seer, and once inside, Freya demanded the seer give Otta a memory potion to learn of his lineage so that he could save his home and his lands."

"And did the seer do that?"

"*Ja*, not only did she do it, the potion revealed that Otta was a direct descendent of Frey, Freya's own brother. This, of course, meant he could keep his land and all his possessions. He was a man of great standing. So he returned to Earth to live out his days happily."

"I thought you said it was a love story." She set her hand tentatively on the curve of Haakon's hip, the warmth of his flesh seeping into her palm and fingers. Thankfully, her shivering had subsided. She was indeed coming back to life.

"It *is* a love story," he whispered. "It is about two souls living in different realms who find each other, who worship, help, and respect each other. And of course, when Otta had lived a full and happy life, he was taken by Freya to her great hall, Sessrumnir, where he still sits today, at her side, as her lover and her equal."

"'As her lover and equal'?"

"*Ja*, they are lovers now. Utterly devoted to each other." He paused. "Freya is not just beautiful, but also powerful and magical and skilled in many things. Just like you are."

"You did not want to marry me for my hunting skills and I am certainly not magical."

"It is true, I wanted you because to me, you are like Freya is to Otta. I loved you the minute I saw you, my beautiful Kenna. If you wish for me to create a stone shrine and make sacrifices to you, then I will."

"That will not be necessary." She curled her fingers into his hip a little. "No one has ever called me 'beautiful' before."

"Then this entire village is foolish. And it is good my men and I are here."

She giggled, just a little. "I don't think anyone in Tillicoulty is foolish."

"You are beautiful and special," he said, running his hand up her arm, to her shoulder, then back to her wrist again.

Everywhere he touched left a trail of warm sensation. A shiver of a different kind traveled over her skin.

"I just need you to understand how I feel, Kenna. I need you to promise not to run from me again."

"I don't know if I can promise that."

He frowned and swallowed, closing his eyes for a moment as if thinking. "If I hadn't pulled you from the water, then—"

"I am glad you did, but I wouldn't have *needed* saving had you not been chasing me."

"I wasn't chasing you."

"That was how it felt." Her shoulders stiffened in frustration. "You forced me to marry you. A man I don't know. A man who only committed to my God yesterday. And then you want to bed me, plant your seed. Of course I ran." She glared at him. "Wouldn't Freya have run too? Wouldn't she have done everything she could to get away?"

"You are right she would have." He nodded, regretting being the cause of her frustration. "I am lucky not to have been turned into a boar for all eternity."

"What I am trying to say," Kenna went on, ignoring the hint of a smile tugging his lips, "is that I have spent my whole life proving that I'm just as capable as my brother, as Bryce, and the other boys, now men, in Tillicoulty. I can hunt and track and swim and run as well as they all can. I can help build a boat, sail and fish too. And while they have never had to prove themselves, they also have never had to worry about a Norseman getting washed up on the beach and claiming them."

"You... You wish to be a boy?" His eyes widened.

"What? No...I wouldn't want that, wouldn't want one of..." She paused and again was aware of his cock between them. It wasn't completely soft now and she could feel the tip, with the ring, pressing on her leg. "I wouldn't want the appendage you have. It appears very uncomfortable."

He chuckled and slipped his hand between their bodies, shifting his cock and moving his hips. "It is true a cock is the downfall of some men. Some use it like a brain, and others become incapacitated when struck violently upon it. The excruciating pain gives their enemy enough time to wield their sword."

Kenna shifted so her head was on the pillow next to his. She pulled up the fur, glad to be more like herself, though her feet still felt like they had pins jabbing at them.

"That is one reason I don't wish to be a boy," she went on. "The other is that I'm as good a fighter and hunter as any man. More so, for I can be quieter, lighter, faster at times. I have good eyes and good hearing and I'm more patient. I do not wish to be seen as weaker than you, seen as a poor, weak girl in need of saving and caring for."

"I understand." He tucked a strand of hair behind her ear.

"Do you?"

"*Ja*, Viking women would say the same thing to any man who wanted to marry them. Look at my sister, Astrid—she is skilled and independent and likes to be seen as such."

Kenna was pleased he understood but also surprised. Was he telling the truth? "So you will let me hunt?"

"*Ja*."

"And fish?"

"*Ja*." He paused. "Of course."

"Good."

"So you are staying?"

"It depends."

His face was so close to hers, she could see every swirl and lick of the neck tattoo that ended around his jawline where his stubble began.

"On what?" he asked.

"If you will see me as your equal." It was a bold demand of a Viking—one who had been a monster to her yesterday, the stuff of nightmares the day before.

"My love," he said softly, his eyebrows pulling low. "Why would I see you as anything else? Of course you are my equal."

Her throat tightened with emotion. "Do you mean that? Really?"

"You have seen the two new chairs outside our bedchamber. They are of equal size. We will rule as equals, King and Queen of Tillicoulty, and one day, our lands may expand and so will our people. We will consult on matters, consider each other's thoughts. I could not do it without you. Every king needs a clever, kind, and brave queen. Me even more so, for I am in a foreign land."

"I didn't think. I..." She lifted her hand to hover by his cheek for a moment and then dropped it to her side again. "I thought when you wanted to marry me, you just wanted my body, a supply of heirs, a slave to do your bidding, cleaning, and cooking."

"That is not our way. That is not the Viking way. Where I am from, women are valued as much as men. Shield-maidens are as important in battle as warriors, and queens can rule alone, without a king, if they should wish."

"That is true?"

"I promise, in the name of God, it is." He drew his face closer. His gaze was intense, as though he were seeing right into her mind. His words had filled her soul with warmth the way his flesh had heated her body. He surrounded her, filled her, and it felt more good than bad.

Her fear of him was slipping away. He'd saved her at great peril to himself. And now he wished them to be equals.

"Please don't run from me again," he whispered, sliding his hand up to cup her nape. "I couldn't bear to lose you, not now I've finally found you."

"If you treat me as an equal, I won't run," she said quietly, her attention slipping to his wide mouth. "I will stay, here, with you."

"And this is where I want you. Right here." He pressed his lips to hers, soft but firm, warm and pliant.

She moaned. Her first kiss was surprisingly pleasant, considering it was a Viking kissing her.

He pulled back slightly and with his eyes closed, he murmured something in a language she didn't understand.

"What did you say?" she whispered.

"My heart beats for you and only you." He kissed her again. This time, his slick tongue poked into her mouth and touched hers.

She closed her eyes, her heart rate picked up further, and she curled her toes. A strange, tugging sensation caught her nipples and she pressed her thighs together when the sensation dipped lower.

His breath blew on her cheek and he slanted his head, deepening the kiss. His cock grew harder, pressing into her as he pulled her closer.

She broke the kiss. "Haakon. I do not know how it is in your world, but…"

"But?"

"I am… untouched."

He frowned and swiped his tongue over his bottom lip. "'Untouched'?"

"Aye, it is how it should be, how God says it should be on a wedding night."

"I don't understand."

She'd have to spell it out. "I am a virgin, Haakon. No man has even kissed me before, let alone…"

"A virgin. Surely, you have had nights of pleasure during the long winter moons? What else is there to do?"

"No." She scowled at the very suggestion.

"But I… Not even that one, that man…Bryce? I see how he looks at you."

"Bryce! No. Definitely not and he doesn't look at me like anything. He's a friend is all."

"Oh, he does *look* at you. I know my competition." He traced the length of her nose with the tip of his finger, then over her lips and to her chin. He kept her face lifted to his. "He wishes to be more than a friend."

"It is not what I wish."

"But you wish to be more than *my* friend?" He raised his eyebrows.

"It seems I am already more than your friend, that is what you insisted upon in return for the safety of my people. I would sacrifice anything for their lives, including my own."

"Your willingness to sacrifice is honorable, another thing that makes me desire you so."

"You desire me…now?" Her stomach clenched at the thought of him entering her, of planting his seed with his big, pierced cock. She ached from her brush with death and her muscles pained her from shivering. She was sure his wild bedding routine would finish her off entirely.

"I desire nothing more than to enter you right now and stay there until night falls and day breaks again, until we are both exhausted from pleasure and our bodies slick with sweat, but…" He pulled back and tucked the fur closer around her neck. "Your ankle needs attention and I know that you need warm broth and rest."

She nodded stiffly, relief washing over her, but at the same time, she was intrigued at the thought of him entering her and giving her sweaty pleasure. "That is true. I am not quite fully recovered."

"But maybe," he said.

"Aye?"

"No. It is not how it should be."

"What isn't?"

"I was going to tell you it will happen this night, that you should prepare yourself for me. But I wish to prove that we are equals and so…" His jaw tensed and he stood from the bed. His cock was hard and long, tapping up against his abdomen.

"So?" She tore her attention from his erection, a quiver going through her.

"So we will not join as one until you are ready. Until you instigate it." He clamped his lips tightly and then sniffed, his nostrils flaring.

"But…what if I never…?" Which was a distinct possibility. "Want you."

"Then I will not have lawful heirs." He turned and reached for his pants. "Which will pain me enormously, but if it saves you pain, saves you from doing something you do not want to do, then it will be worth it. I will bear it." He paused and threw his hand upward. "And I am sure my new God will give me strength as I forsake all other women for my tight-legged wife."

She stared at him, not knowing what to say. He'd stolen any words she might have thrown at him. Never in all eternity would she have thought her new giant of a Viking husband would commit to such a thing.

Surely, he was lying.

He reached for his tunic, dragged it on, then threw another log on the fire. "Wait there, in the warmth. I will return with broth and tincture for your ankle. I don't know where Astrid has got to."

Chapter Seventeen

One Week Later

"SO TELL ME, Noah, who is this King Athol who claims he rules my land?" Haakon jabbed at his bare chest, his biceps bulging around his arm ring and his muscles flexing. "My land!"

The Great House was overly warm, the central open hearth aglow with embers, and the air held the pleasing scent of onions, herbs, and smoke. Haakon had removed his tunic some time ago when his underarms had prickled with heat and he had settled down to establish facts with his new people.

His beautiful Kenna sat at his side holding a goblet of ale. The bandage had gone from her ankle and she wore a new blue, woolen gown her mother had made her. She also wore a boar fang necklace that matched his, something he'd sourced while she'd been recovering from her near-death experience in the river. She'd seemed pleased with it and that had pleased him. He only wanted to see her smile, for it made his heart warm.

"King Athol is from the Eastlands," Noah said, wiping his warm brow, "and inherited the title from his father, King Harold."

Haakon studied his new father by marriage. Their relationship was gaining trust, not least because Kenna had confirmed to Noah that Haakon had indeed cared for her when she had been at her most vulnerable and injured. "And is King Athol like his father?"

"No, his father was a quiet ruler. He liked peace and stability. He was also a very pious man, believing his crown had been given to him by God."

"He thought God gave him his crown?"

"Aye, his destiny, I suppose," Noah added.

"As you believe it is your destiny to be king here," Kenna said, turning to Haakon. "Am I wrong?"

"No, you are not wrong. It is my destiny to be here with you." He squeezed her small hand, enjoying the fact that she didn't flinch anymore when he touched her. Not that he'd touched her much. Each night, he'd hoped she'd reach for him and be wet and willing, but so far, she'd huddled under the furs on their bed and turned her back to him.

"King Athol is not a quiet ruler," Olaf said, joining the conversation. "He demands many *cáin* to fund his army and his boat building."

"And each year, the price goes up." Noah tutted and shook his head.

"You must pay him *cáin*, and what do you get in return?" Haakon asked. "When this is your land. *Our* land."

"He claims the forest is his," Kenna said. "The ocean too. Which means all the boars, rabbits, and pheasants, as well as the fish, belong to him. He charges us for hunting, foraging, and fishing."

"When it is your own skill and weapon?" Haakon could feel his irritation rising, and not just because another man believed himself King of Tillicoulty.

"Aye." Hamish nodded and glanced at Astrid, who was sitting away from the group carving arrowheads. "And when it is our ancestors who have lived and died here. If it is anyone's land and sea, it is ours." Hamish folded his arms and puffed up his chest.

"I agree." Haakon stood and helped himself to more ale. He also glanced at Astrid, who had been silent throughout the entire meeting. "And because I agree, I... We..." He gestured to Gunner, Knud, Ivar, Egil, and Orm, who were sitting at a bench munching on bread and cold meat. "We will fight with you when he next visits. We will defeat him and claim our land back and knock his crown from his head."

"We do not wish to fight?" Noah said tilting his chin. "That would end very badly."

"How many men does he bring to collect his dues?" Haakon sat back down and directed the question at Kenna.

"He visits once a year, and not with an army." She paused and rubbed her chin, something he'd noticed she did when thinking. "A handful. Ten, twenty at most."

"And they are soldiers?"

"A mixture of soldiers, servants, sometimes family members, and of course a bursar."

"And when is he next due?"

"In the early weeks of summer," Olaf said. "He always visits when the weather is fine and before the midges start biting."

"Good, that gives us plenty of time to ensure everyone is armed and trained." He nodded at Orm. "Don't you think?"

Orm shrugged and shoved pork into his mouth, chewing noisily. "*Ja*, I guess. But unless we kill them all and dispose of the bodies, there'll be more right behind looking for their king."

Haakon thought for a moment. "If I kill the king, I want everyone to know, I won't hide our victory."

"And risk bloody revenge?" Kenna asked.

"Our neighbors might be pleased he is dead." Haakon nodded. "*Ja?*"

"And if they are not?" Noah asked.

"Then it is the perfect way to let them know who the new king is and expand our territories."

"We don't need more land—we have enough. We just need to stop paying to use what is ours," Kenna said.

"I understand that, wife, but if we expand, it could be us collecting *cáin*." As soon as he'd said it, he knew it had been a mistake.

Her eyebrows pulled low and her eyes flashed. "And so you would make yourself as immoral and hated as King Athol? Charging for services that are not yours to give?"

"I think it's a great idea," Astrid suddenly said. "The more gold, silver, and treasure we can gather, the better. I will fight, I will kill, and I will collect our dues."

"Why?" Olaf asked. "Why would you want so much?"

"To take to Valhalla, of course." She frowned at Olaf. "I, for one, wish to be rich in the afterlife. I wish to be rich and pampered and surrounded by luxury."

Olaf crossed himself. "There is no need for material possessions in heaven, or I suspect in Valhalla."

"Do not speak of Valhalla, old man." Astrid stood, sprinkles of wood shavings dropping from her pants to the floor. "You know nothing about it, and you will never go there, for only brave, strong warriors are permitted entry. You... You will rot in the ground with the worms and slugs when you die, nothing more than that. This is something I can assure you."

"*Astrid!*" Haakon snapped.

Orm laughed and Gunnar joined in now that he was picking up the new language and could piece together what Astrid had said.

"I speak the truth, brother." Astrid pointed at Haakon, her eyes flashing dangerously. Her temper was flaring like a torch to a pyre; her cheeks were pink and her fists clenched. "And you...Haakon...you will also rot in the ground, the great All Father will see to it, and when you stand at the gates of Valhalla and claim you are a great warrior, the gods will turn you away, the wolves that guard the mighty gates will chase you away. For they are ashamed of you also and then—"

"*Astrid!*" Haakon stood and slammed down his drink. His chest puffed up in frustration that she'd dared to speak this way to him. "Enough!"

It didn't put her off her tirade. "The gods have served you well, protected you, guided you with the runes, and still, you forsake them for a god who has never taken a step into battle with you, and for what?" She pointed at Kenna and wrinkled her nose. "A mere woman. A foreign woman who poked you on the beach? It is the most dishonorable thing you could have done to them." She flicked her loose hair over her shoulders, the orange of the flames dancing in the red strands. "Father would cringe if he found out and Ravn…he would laugh and say this is why he got to be King of Drangar. Because you are not worthy."

"Watch your mouth, sister of mine!" Haakon roared. "You insult me *and* the queen."

She slammed her hands onto her hips. "Do I look as if I fucking care?" She threw a withering look at Kenna and then around the group of village men, her attention settling on Hamish. "You are all underdogs, failures, and I cannot stay here, in a place where my gods are ignored, worse than that, treated as though they are nothing more than fleas on wool."

"That is not how it is," Orm said, standing. "And you know it. We love our gods and—"

"Oh, it is like that and it's what I see. When did you last ask me for a rune stone reading, Orm? Or any of you? Gunnar, Ivar, Knud…it is as though you forget your gods and the paths they have planned for you. Egil is usually a man to give many offerings, yet he has given none for days, have you?"

Before Egil could answer, she grabbed her bow and arrow and stormed past the open hearth. "I am leaving this wicked place. Do not come searching for me. Consider me dead." She opened the door, letting in a stiff wind, then left the building, not shutting it behind her.

"Astrid," Kenna called.

But she was gone.

Ivar got up and closed the door.

Haakon reckoned he, Egil, and Knud only understood half of what she'd said, but it had been enough to know she was very unhappy.

"Where will she go?" Hamish asked with a frown.

"I do not care." Haakon waved his arm in the air. "She wanted a new life, new lands, yet she cannot adjust to new ways. She is a fool with a closed mind." He sat heavily, frustration coursing through him.

"Husband," Kenna said, reaching out and resting her small hand on his forearm. "Should you go to your sister? She does seem very upset."

It was the first time Kenna had instigated a touch between them and instantly, all thoughts of Astrid and her scorn flew from his mind. All he could think of was Kenna's warm fingers, the pressure of her palm, the concern in her eyes. "No," he managed. "I do not need to go to her."

"Are you sure?"

"*Ja*, she has a temper worse than a bear woken midwinter by a swarm of bees. It is best she calm down before anyone speaks to her."

Hamish stood and threw a thick log onto the hearth. Hot flakes of ash flew upward. "She has a tongue as sharp as a dagger."

"That is true." Haakon dragged his attention from his wife's hand. "And a wildness no man has yet to tame."

"'Tame'?" Hamish drew down his eyebrows and studied Haakon. "Why would she need taming?"

Orm chuckled. "What man could live a life full of hot sparks? Marriage to my sister would be a battle every day about something and she's a sure aim with her sword and a wily huntress with her bow. One wrong word in the day, one bedding that didn't find her writhing in ecstasy, and her husband would likely get his balls chopped off and hung up for Odin's ravens to feast upon."

Hamish sat back down with a jolt. He was still frowning as he tapped his fingers together in a fast, fractious rhythm.

Haakon wished he knew what was going on in his brother-by-marriage's head. Was he scared of Astrid? He should be; she'd made it clear she hated all the Lothlenders. Or did he desire her? If so, that was a sure path to his downfall. Astrid would never bed a non-believer.

And if Hamish tried… It would be quite the mess for Haakon to fix.

He supped his ale and turned to Kenna. She'd lifted her hand and Bryce was pouring her another drink.

"Thank you," she said, smiling up at him.

Haakon's stomach tightened. He didn't like Bryce one bit and liked it even less when the man found excuses to be near Kenna.

"Would you like some fish, Your Grace?" Bryce said, biting on his bottom lip as though holding in a laugh.

Kenna *did* laugh. "Don't call me that."

"Why shouldn't he?" Haakon snapped. "For you are queen."

"It's just…" Bryce straightened and shrugged. "Not many men grew up with their queen the way I did. We used to run through the forest chasing rabbits, collect clams from dawn till dusk, carve gifts for each other and sometimes, on the warmest days, frolic naked in the waves of Eliah Bay."

Haakon felt the pressure in his head double and it had already been high after Astrid's outburst. "What?"

Bryce chuckled, clearly knowing he'd irked Haakon.

"We only did that once," Kenna said quickly. "In the waves, and we were young, so young. My father scolded us, said the current would take us out to sea."

"Was it only once?" Bryce said, knocking back a gulp of ale. "Or was it many times over many summers?"

"Only once when we were so young." Kenna scowled at him. "Please, fill up my father's and Olaf's goblets."

Bryce raised his eyebrows. "Of course, Your Grace." He settled his attention on Haakon for a moment then turned away.

Haakon's instincts told him that look had been a challenge. That Bryce was covering up a deep hate for his king, which surmounted to treason, and Haakon should challenge him on it.

But not today. Not when his beautiful wife was just beginning to soften around the edges. A battle to the death with her childhood friend would definitely set him back a few steps when Bryce was left bloody and lifeless outside the fort wall.

"He needs to be careful," Haakon said, more to himself than Kenna.

She heard him. "Bryce?"

"Aye, he disrespects you."

"It's just his way." She shrugged to make light of it. "We've jested many times over the years."

"He needs to learn everything is different now." Haakon banged his chest. "I am here and you are mine."

"As if I could forget that?" She raised her eyebrows at him and lifted her chin. "Every moment of every day from dawn till dusk." She paused. "You are there."

"As it should be."

She turned away and he studied her delicate but proud profile. The surge of jealousy he had whenever Bryce was in sight was real and intoxicating. He wanted Kenna to himself. He wanted to bed her, to be as one with her. Perhaps when...*if*...that happened, he'd be less irritated by the boy she'd known in childhood who now looked at her as though he wanted to lick her all over.

Licking Kenna all over was his job!

Chapter Eighteen

Kenna swung up onto Sal, her favorite Highland pony, and turned her in a circle. "We'll ride up to Partridge Point. You can see all of our land from there."

"I would like that," Haakon said, seating himself on Fen, the biggest and strongest horse the village had—his duties were usually confined to pulling the plow.

Kenna hoped Fen would behave himself.

But the moment she saw Haakon gather the reins and adjust himself in the saddle, it was clear he was an accomplished horseman and her worries were eased.

They rode out of the fort, Haakon throwing a wave to Ivar, who was keeping watch today.

"Your men seem to have settled here," Kenna remarked, leading them toward a woodland track that climbed steeply.

"*Ja*, they are content and learning the language."

"Were they not content at Drangar?"

He twisted his mouth a little and shrugged. "I guess not, or they wouldn't have left with me."

"They have no family there?" She'd been curious about Gunner, Knud, Egil, and Ivar for several days—since she'd stopped fearing them, that was. They were all big—especially Gunner—and tattooed, grunty, and brash.

Haakon chuckled. "They did not have wives, if that is what you mean, though Gunner had one once. She died of fever."

"I am sorry for Gunner." Poor Gunner. What a tragedy for his heart.

"It was a hard time for him, and many others. Fever swept through our people. It took the weakest. Perhaps that's why the gods send such diseases, so only the strongest survive."

"I believe God is merciful. The fever is a wicked spell sent by the Devil."

"The Devil?"

"Aye." She took to the track and ducked beneath a branch. "His trickery and evil knows no bounds. He will stop at nothing to tempt and deceive and then claim your soul into hell for all of eternity."

"He is someone you fear?"

"As should you, though he is not a *someone*. He comes in many guises."

Haakon was quiet.

"I thought you were the Devil," she said, throwing him a glance and tightening her cloak at her chin. "When I saw you on the beach that day."

"You did?"

"Aye. I was frightened of you and what you might do."

"I'm sorry to frighten you." He frowned and moved a pliant fir branch out of his way. "Do I still frighten you?"

She considered him—big and broad, his dark fur heavy across his shoulders and his hair un-brushed and hanging long. There was a wildness about him. Feral. A fierce warrior lurked just beneath the surface. She felt sure he'd fought, maimed, killed, in his life, yet no, she wasn't scared of him, not now. "You have only shown me your gentle side, Haakon. So no, I am not scared of you."

"Good." He smiled, something he did often in her presence. "I do not want you to be scared of me. I will never hurt you, only protect you."

She nodded. "I'm trying to believe that."

"You should," he said earnestly. "And I will prove it not just with words, but with actions. This time next year, you will believe it to the core of your soul."

She smiled. "Tell me more about Drangar. I know that the land is dark for many weeks. What is the land like?"

"It is poor land for farming. The cliffs rise from the fjords, straight up. There is no soil to plant, and where there is soil, around the port of Drangar, the land is frozen solid for much of the year. We only have one chance of crops before the frost comes again, and if rain or animals destroy our crops, then it is a hungry winter for everyone. People die when the harvest is poor."

"And that is why you are interested in our crops?"

"You are so much farther south and you have sun all year round. The earth is cold but still provides. I am keen to see every season and learn your farming ways."

"And you will be shown, Haakon. Noah has promised that. Already, he demonstrated Fen pulling the plow."

"Great invention." Haakon nodded. "It was worth almost drowning out at sea just to see that."

She laughed. "I am glad it pleased you so."

"I like it when you do that."

"What?" The track leveled out and the trees began to thin. A squirrel scampered up a tree, a quick flash of red. "What do you like that I do?"

"Laugh. It's a lovely sound and fills me with warmth even on as cold a day as this."

Her cheeks heated, as they often did when he complimented her. "Haakon. Must you say such things?"

He chuckled.

"So why did your brother and sister leave Drangar?" She wanted to change the subject. "And what did your mother think about all of you leaving?"

He blew out a breath and looked around, the vista spreading before them. "My mother died many years ago."

"I am sorry for your loss."

"Thank you."

"But I find it hard to believe Astrid and Orm could leave your father and brother. You, I understand, your brother had fought you for the crown, but them...?"

"Not really hard to understand." Haakon shrugged and came alongside her now that they were off the narrow track. "Orm has never had a good relationship with my father."

"Why not?"

"Many years ago, at the sacred Festival of Uppsala, when allegiance and fealty is shown to the gods in the form of sacrifices, Orm refused."

"Refused? Refused what?"

"He was chosen to be one of nine young males to die, to go to the gods and dine with them. But Orm didn't want to. He said he had things to do on Earth. My father was horribly shamed by him. Orm had broken the rules of the gods in order to live a life of parties and women here on Earth. All his life, my father strived to be noticed by the gods, to be in their favor, but Orm had gotten the family noticed for the wrong reasons, for disrespect and disloyalty."

"I can understand why he didn't want to die to appease gods he has never seen." She fought down a bitter taste of disbelief and disgust at this ritual. "Did you feel that he had shamed you also?"

"No, nor did Astrid. An unwilling sacrifice is a bad omen for everyone. He would reach the gods' realm with sagas of misery and corruption." He shrugged and drew his horse to a halt at the edge of a steep drop. "And maybe I'm selfish, but I didn't want my youngest brother to not be in my life. He is an...an acquired taste, but there is love in his heart."

"Underneath the madness." Kenna also came to a halt and she stared out at the forest and the sea beyond. In the distance, small islands seemed to hover on the horizon.

"Madness." Haakon shook his head. "He is not mad—he simply sees the world differently than others do. And he is amused easily. Humor comes fast and is occasionally inappropriate, but I'd rather that than constant misery, for that is how Ravn is. Always bad-tempered about something, striving for the next thing to claim, even when he has plenty of everything already."

"I am glad my brother is not like that."

"Hamish is a good man." Haakon nodded and delved into his cloak. "And he is a good son and brother, I have seen that."

"He is. I love him very much."

"As you should."

An eagle soared about them. Its wings grew still as it caught the air, the feathered tips like spread fingers.

"I have a gift for you," Haakon said, passing her a wooden cross.

"You have?" She leaned from the saddle to take it. It had been carved intricately and was a replica of the larger one on the wall of their bedchamber. "It is lovely." The wood had been polished smooth and she ran her finger over the curved ends, following the grooved pattern.

"I know you like this symbol," he said.

"It is the cross that our savior, Jesus Christ, died upon."

"He died on it? You said he was nailed to it."

"Aye, crucified. He died up there for our sins."

"A sacrifice?"

She paused and bit on her bottom lip, thinking of Orm's unwillingness to sacrifice himself for the Norse gods. "Aye, I suppose it is like that."

"I understand now," Haakon said, nodding at the vista. "What is that? Out there?"

"That is Orc. It is an island with a small population. Occasionally, we trade with them and the smaller isles farther north." She slipped the small cross into her pocket, feeling unexpectedly pleased with the thoughtful little gift, just as she had with the boar fang necklace he'd given her.

"Your boats are small for such a journey in these seas," Haakon said.

"That is why we only trade occasionally with them." She shrugged and pushed away the worry that she and her mother had gone through the last time her father and Hamish had taken to the seas. They'd been gone for three weeks, much longer than anticipated.

"And to the west?" Haakon asked.

"You would walk for three days before another settlement. And it is only small. It is over a week's walk to a larger one."

"So all this land I can see belongs to Tillicoulty?"

"Until King Athol shows up demanding rent, then aye, it does."

He frowned, his eyebrows pulling low. "A man who passes through once a year has no claim. He is little more than a wanderer."

There was something in Haakon's determined tone that stirred hope within Kenna. Her new husband was not a man to be messed with, and King Athol, even though he had yet to show his face in Tillicoulty this year, had clearly messed with Haakon already.

"I agree," she said, studying the way his eyes flashed. "He shouldn't have a claim."

"I am glad we see it the same." He leaned forward in the saddle, stretching out his back. "Because we are as one. King and queen. If we fall, we fall together, but when we rise, we will rise together and take our people with us."

"You really believe these are your people now?"

"With all of my heart." He pressed his fist to his chest. "This is my home now and they are good people, worth fighting for…worth dying for."

Her heart did a strange flip. He spoke the truth. She could see the passion in his eyes, hear it in his voice.

Were they better off now that the Vikings had arrived? Had their biggest fear for so long proven to be their salvation?

Perhaps that was the case. Perhaps they should have prayed for them sooner.

A squally gust caught her hair, whipping it over her face. It was quickly followed by a bluster of tiny snowflakes.

Haakon looked up. "We have been so busy looking out to sea, we didn't notice the black clouds coming from the mountains in the east."

"We should head back." Kenna turned her horse and ducked her face from the biting wind. "The weather has been kind this morn, but it could turn any moment."

Haakon followed her onto the track, his horse shaking its head and snorting as though eager to get back and munch hay in the barn.

AN HOUR LATER, they were riding under the watchtower and into the village.

"Shall I take your horse?" Bryce asked, appearing from behind a chicken coop. "It is nearly dark." The wind was trying to rip his cloak from his shoulders. Flicking and flapping it as if in a foul temper.

Kenna slipped from the saddle, landing softly on the hard ground. Lass was slinking around her legs in an instant. "Thanks, Bryce," she said over a clap of thunder.

He nodded and took the reins, head ducked against the driving snow.

Haakon ignored Bryce and carried on riding.

"I have to speak to my mother," Kenna called to Haakon's stiff back as she ruffled Lass's ears and gripped her fur closer to her chest.

Haakon didn't answer. And she knew why. Whenever Bryce was around, it was as though her husband had nettle rash; he was prickly and irritable.

But Haakon suddenly pulled his horse to a halt. "Who are you?" he called to his right.

Kenna narrowed her eyes against the weather. A stooped figure was huddled against the wind and rain beside the pigpen wall, hood pulled up and a gnarly cane in his hand. She didn't recognize him, either.

Quickly, she walked forward. There was a stranger in their midst. Her hackles rose, her suspicion alive.

"I said, *who are you?*" Haakon shouted above a particularly violent gust. "Answer me."

The stranger turned. He was a weathered, old man with a tangled, gray beard and a patch over one eye. "Forgive me." He held up a shaky hand. "I am but a wanderer and I find myself wandering here on this pitiful night."

"And what name do you go by, wanderer?" Kenna asked.

"McFadden of Goul," he said, tightening his hood so that only his visible eye peered out.

"*Your Grace*," Haakon snapped. "You are addressing the Queen of Tillicoulty. You will show her respect."

"I beg your forgiveness." He ducked his head low as though bowing. "Your Grace."

Kenna tipped her chin and set down her shoulders. It felt odd to do it. She'd been an ordinary woman such a short time ago, yet now she was queen and addressed as such.

"And I am king. King Haakon. You are trespassing on my land."

"I just wish for some stale bread and ale." He dipped lower, seeming to be trying to make himself smaller and even more pathetic. "The man on the watchtower gave me permission to ask."

"Of course you can and—" Kenna started.

"And what do we get in return?" Haakon demanded, holding his horse still. Fen was restless to get to shelter and hoofed the ground. "What can you offer a king when you clearly have nothing?"

"Ah, great king, I can give you what I see here." He tapped his eye patch. "Since the raven took my eye, I have a gift for seeing into the future. I can spot a sea of trouble, a meadow of hay, a pack of wolves lying in wait. I will tell you what you must prepare for, what you need not fear, and whom here you can truly trust. That is a gift, indeed, is it not?"

"A raven took your eye." Haakon peered more closely at the man, his hair whipping about his face. "That is what happened to Odin."

The wanderer said nothing and held still under Haakon's curious gaze.

"Well, come on, then." Haakon gestured to the Great House. "Come with me. But you must tell me everything you see. I want to know it all." He turned his horse again and kicked it on.

The old man scuttled along behind him, his cane splashing in the puddles.

"Mother," Kenna said, ducking into the home she'd lived all of her life until the last few weeks. "Guess what?"

"Kenna. I am glad you are back. There is a storm coming."

"It has already arrived." Kenna pulled off her wet fur and hung it on a hook. "The wind is trying to shake the branches from the trees. But guess what? A one-eyed wanderer has also blown in. He is a seer and is with Haakon right now."

"Another wanderer. May God have mercy on their souls. Here, warm by the fire." Her mother stirred a pot of broth. "And eat something. You are quite pale."

"I am well. I just want to know what the wanderer will say." Kenna rubbed her palms before the flames. They'd become chilled and stiff from holding the reins. "'Haps I should—"

"Child, sit, and warm up. Where is your husband and this wanderer?"

"They have gone to the Great House."

"He must eat some of this. Your husband, the king, must keep up his strength to protect our village."

"There is food there, at the Great House."

"Has Astrid cooked?"

"I told you, we have not seen her for days."

"That is a worry." Her mother ladled broth into an earthenware bowl. "And strange, because Hamish has also been gone for several days."

"He has?"

"Aye." She shrugged. "But he said he was going trapping in the mountains and it is not unknown for him to sleep outdoors."

"Not in the winter." Kenna frowned and looked at Hamish's cot in the corner. It was strewn with furs and an old pair of boots sat beside it. A wooden cross hung on the wall.

"He can look after himself. I am not worried."

Kenna couldn't help but be worried. She was also worried about Astrid, who didn't know this land. Much as Haakon was frustrated with his sister, Kenna knew he loved her.

"I am worried about you." Kenna's mother sat opposite her on a small bench and cupped her own bowl of broth.

"Why? I am here and safe."

"You are so pale. Are you with child already?"

"What!" Kenna nearly choked on her broth. "No, it has been hardly any time since we were married and—"

"It has been known to happen quickly and…and maybe Bryce…did you ever?"

"No!" Kenna's mouth hung open and her eyes widened.

"Well, I did wonder." She studied Kenna thoughtfully. "He looks at you as if—"

"No, of course not. Never. Not with Bryce." She shook her head. "It's impossible, and it would be a sin. We were not married and…and actually, it's impossible for me to be pregnant by anyone, for I am still a virgin."

"Still a virgin?" Her mother set her food aside.

"Aye."

Her mother touched her fingers to her lips, tapping them thoughtfully. "But...But you are a married woman. You have a husband in your bed."

"Aye, but that doesn't mean anything."

"It should mean *everything*."

"Have you seen him, Mother? Have you seen my husband?" Kenna gestured to the door. "The size of him. He is a brute, a Norse brute who claimed me for his own with no care what I thought about the whole thing."

"It doesn't sound like there has been any claiming." Her mother shook her head. "I don't understand."

Kenna frowned. "Do you need to understand?"

"I'd like to. I am your mother, after all."

"He... He..." Kenna sighed and stared at the dancing flames of the fire in front of her. "He didn't want to force himself on me. Said he'd wait until I said I was ready. And even if I never am, he'll stay at my side as a devoted husband."

Her mother was wide-eyed. "Well, I never." She crossed herself. "God does work in mysterious ways."

"What do you mean?"

"He turned up here and we all thought he was a murdering monster and now this... Now you tell me this..."

"'This'?"

"Aye. His conversion to Christianity has clearly given him morals, respect, and consideration. How utterly blessed we are."

Kenna supposed he had been considerate, patient too. Respect? Aye, she couldn't deny he did seem to respect her, as a woman, a queen, and his wife.

"But it is not right, Kenna. A woman must lie with her husband. It is God's will."

"Even if she doesn't want to?"

Her mother tipped her head. "Why don't you want to? From what I see, he treats you well."

"Because… Because I…" She glanced at the door, as though seeing over the wintery ground, past the pigpens, the hay store, and the stone well to where he was talking with the wanderer in their warm home.

She imagined him eating bread and drinking ale, all big and brooding, his hair tousled and his cheeks nipped red by the wind. She breathed deep and was reminded of his masculine smell mixed with the sweet chestnut soap he'd made. And his blue eyes, the way they looked at her. As though he were trying to read her every thought, every dream, every memory. It filled her with warmth.

"He is a good man, Kenna," her mother said quietly.

Kenna cleared her throat. "He still believes in his gods, you know."

"Of course he does." Her mother picked up her food again and stirred it with a spoon. "And it could be they are real."

"What? How can you possibly think that?"

"'Haps God Almighty, our worshipful creator, knew that the Norsemen would need more controlling than the rest of his flock. Maybe He created this Odin and Thor they speak of to keep your husband and his friends from bringing the end of the world."

"God created other gods?" Kenna was aghast at the idea.

"Lesser gods, not as important as angels or even saints, and confined to the north. But powerful enough to control the monsters who rape and pillage our land."

"You just said Haakon *wasn't* a monster…didn't you?"

"He is redeemed. And he is your husband." She nodded at Kenna's food. "I suggest you finish that and go to him. Do your duty as a wife."

"But I—"

"Lie with him, Kenna. It is time."

Kenna gritted her teeth, though she couldn't deny the flush of warmth that went from her core to her breasts and then settled between her legs.

"A man needs to find satisfaction, and a man such as yours more often than others," her mother went on. "And the way he looks at you, daughter of mine, the way his eyes follow you around the room, the way he smiles if you smile, anticipates your next drink or meal, and..."

"Gives me gifts?" She held the cross up. The one he'd given her earlier.

Her mother nodded approvingly. "Aye, and gives you gifts, I suspect he'll be a man who will make sure you also have satisfaction in bed."

"If I survive him bedding me, I will be satisfied enough."

"My dearest child." Her mother pressed her palm on Kenna's knee. "I have told you little about coupling—it is God's will that it's the domain of the married woman, not the maiden—but I hope you find pleasure with your husband."

"'Pleasure'?"

"Aye, it makes the burden of carrying a child for nine months much more bearable if there has been pleasure when planting the seed."

"Mother." She set her empty bowl aside. "I have never once presumed the act to be pleasurable. It is something to be endured."

Her mother reached for another log and set it in the flames. "If that is what you truly believe, then go and endure. Put it off no longer."

Kenna stood and swallowed, her throat tight. An image of Haakon's naked body flashed into her mind. Huge and broad, his skin stretched tightly over solid muscle and his pierced cock...long and dark and impossibly big. The image brought with it a fluttery feeling that landed in her stomach and spread tingles to her pussy and hardened her nipples.

"All the women before you have survived this," her mother said quietly. "You will too."

"Aye, but they didn't marry a Viking." Kenna grabbed her fur, slung it over her shoulders, and clasped it tightly beneath her chin.

She stalked into the wild weather, her mind spinning and her body hot with anticipation yet cold with dread.

It was time to be a wife. To be King Haakon's wife.

Chapter Nineteen

As Kenna scurried to the Great House—a private dwelling now, as Haakon had claimed the entire place, leaving the other Vikings to make their own arrangements around the village—she reminded herself that not only was she strong, very capable, and independent, she was also a queen.

Her people respected her.

And her husband...he loved her.

That knowledge had come to her slowly, but now that it had landed, it was thick and strong and poured through her veins, making her heart beat faster. A queen had a duty to do. A queen had to show inner strength as well as physical strength, no matter what the task at hand.

And now it was time to do just that.

She stepped into the warmth and stood for a moment, letting her eyes adjust to the dimness. In the central trough, a fire had burnt low, the embers glowing. A table was set with jugs and mugs, along with a bowl of nuts and dried berries. Several squat, tallow candles were dotted about and a decorative wall hanging consisting of shells and feathers filled the space beside the large chairs she and Haakon sat on when holding meetings and council.

There was no sign of Haakon or the wanderer.

She discarded her cloak and stepped over a chicken that had escaped its coop and appeared to be nesting by the drying sealskins.

The sound of gentle splashing water caught her attention. It was coming from the bedchamber.

She headed toward it, tucking her hair behind her ears. When she pulled the blanket back she was greeted with the sight of Haakon standing before a roaring fire.

He'd stripped off his tunic and wore only his pants. His feet were bare on the fur rug. For a moment, her attention was harnessed by the width of his shoulders and the thickness of his neck. She smoothed her fingertips over her palms, wondering what it would be like to touch his back, explore every dip and rise the way the light of the flames were doing.

Before him, on a table, was a bowl of steaming water. Using his palms, he scooped some up and washed his now-clean-shaven face, scrubbing at it industriously.

Kenna watched, enjoying the fact that he hadn't noticed her arrival. Usually, he was aware of where she was at all times. She also liked how he looked without his dark stubble. His jaw was angled, his chin strong and his lips sensual.

After washing and drying his face, he dragged his hair up, piling the long, dark strands on the top of his head. He then began, with the blade, to hack at the hair still hanging around his ears.

"What are you doing?" she asked, quickly stepping forward as several locks fell unceremoniously to the floor.

He turned. "Kenna. I did not know you were here."

"What are you doing?" she asked again, reaching for his blade and stopping the hewing.

"My hair, it is too long. It's annoying in this wind. And it catches on my clothes. If I wear battle armor, it will be a hindrance." He frowned. "Astrid would usually cut it, plait it, get it out of my way. I figured sawing it off would be the easiest thing, as she is not here."

Kenna stepped up closer and stared into his eyes. "You have me now." She touched the back of her finger to his face. "I will do it for you, husband."

"You will?" His gaze was intense and a tendon flexed in his cheek.

"Aye."

"In that case, I thank you." He nodded, once, a sharp gesture, then sat on a stool.

Kenna set the blade aside and reached for a sheep bone that had been filed into a comb. Standing behind him, she began to work it through the strands.

His hair was windblown and knotty, but eventually, she had it smooth and as shiny as a hazelnut and hanging down his back.

Haakon sat quiet and still, seemingly mesmerized by the dancing flames before him. Or was it her touch that had calmed the usually restless king?

Now that his hair was manageable, Kenna sectioned off the top into one thick tail that ran from his forehead, over the crown of his head, and to his nape and beyond. She fastened it in several places with strips of thin, black leather.

"Feel," she said, gently reaching for his hand.

He patted his head. "That is good and tight."

"Too tight?"

"No, but...but what about this?" He plucked at the loose hair still hanging over his ears. "This is annoying."

"I will shave that for you."

"You can?"

"I have done my father's and Hamish's many times."

"Ah, that is good." He laughed. "I do not wish to be your first."

Kenna bit on her bottom lip. He *would* be her first, but not when it came to hairstyling.

"Pass me the lye," she said. "And when I have taken off the long strands, I will shave it."

He did as she'd asked and she set to work.

Outside, the wind lashed against the roof. A door rattled somewhere to the east and she was sure there was an owl perched in the corner of the room again. It moved occasionally and she felt its yellow eyes upon her.

On and on, she worked, her breaths and hand steady. Haakon remained quiet, his fingers laced on his lap and his spine straight.

When she'd finished one side, she started on the other and continued until the skin of his scalp was smooth and hair-free.

"What do you think?" she asked, setting the blade and lye aside.

Personally, she liked it. The look suited him. It was smarter than his wild beast style and showed off the intricate ink that ran from the curve of his jawline to his collarbones.

"It's good. You're skilled." He used his fingertips to explore the shaved area. "I chose a wife well."

She smiled and studied his neck. "Why do you have this ink here?"

"Here?" He wrapped his hand around his throat.

"Aye."

"It is so when I am in Valhalla, feasting with the gods, my family and friends will see me from down below. As the Valkyrie raise them up to their new realm, they will see my throat, my chin, and know this is me, for I will have my head raised, feasting and laughing with Odin, Thor, Frey, and Freya. It will be a glorious day and my loved ones will come and sit at my side without delay."

"You do not wish to come to heaven with me?"

"Heaven…ah…" He touched the boar fang hanging at his sternum. It had become a habit of his when she questioned him and he was unsure of the answer. "If that is where you are going, then aye, that is where I will be too."

"Not Valhalla?"

"I hope I will go to heaven with you." His eyes narrowed. "How do you have to die to go there? In battle? At sea?"

"No, you just have to die a good person." She tipped her head and studied him. "A man or woman without sin."

"I will have to try harder, then. For sin seems to have followed me around much of my life."

"You have done nothing that would be considered a sin today." She reached out and touched the right side of his chest, just below his hard, dark nipple.

He cleared his throat and watched her stroke his skin in a small, circular motion.

"Have you?" she asked. "When I wasn't looking?"

"No." His voice was low and dark. "But standing here now, with you looking like the sweetest honey I could ever taste, my body wants to sin in the most delicious of ways."

Her breath hitched and her heart rate picked up. He had that liquid, passion-infused glint in his eyes again. Had he been thinking about bedding her the entire time she'd been styling his hair?

Part of her hoped he had.

"My mother tells me it is not a sin to lie together now we are man and wife."

"We are man and wife. That is true." He pressed his lips together, sucking in a breath as though harnessing control. "But until you want to be bedded by me—"

She spoke before she could change her mind. "I do." She tipped her chin and held his eye contact. "It is time."

"Thanks be to Odin, Thor, and my new Christian God," he murmured.

Suddenly, she was in his arms and his mouth was pressing down on hers. The kiss was fast and urgent and he smelled of soap and tasted of ale. His strength surrounded her and the potent heat of his flesh enveloped her.

"My love," he gasped. "I have prayed for this day."

"God will answer your prayers," she managed as she pressed her hands flat on his chest. "When you are a good Christian."

"I'm a really good Christian," he said gruffly as he swooped down to kiss her again. This time, he slid his hands to her ass and squeezed her butt over her pants. He dragged her up against his solid body and a deep groan rumbled from his chest.

"Wait. Wait," Kenna said, pushing at him. "Slow down…not like…not like this." She was panting and her knees were trembling. A hunger she'd never felt before had opened up within her and needed sating.

"But…you said…?"

"I know, and I meant it." She stepped back. "But I am a queen, you made me so, and as such, I will be in control." She tried to inject authority into her voice. It wasn't easy with a huge, horny Viking looking at her as though she were his next meal. "So go and sit on the bed and let me come to you."

Her ass was still tingling where he'd grasped her buttocks and his taste lingered on her lips.

"You want me to go and sit on the bed?" He raised one eyebrow.

"Aye." She held in a smirk. He'd promised her she'd have to beg, yet he was succumbing to her so easily. "I do."

"You do know that if you were any other woman, I'd be buried deep by now. Pounding hard." He paused. "You'd be screaming my name and crying for more."

"I am *not* any other woman." She frowned.

He chuckled. "And don't I know it."

"So do as I said." She pointed to the bed. "King Haakon."

His left shoulder lifted in a half-shrug, then he turned and went to the bed. In the shadows of the corner, Kenna spotted the yellow gaze of an owl. It seemed they'd have an audience for their first time.

He paused and shoved at his pants, revealing his pale buttocks and the dimples in his lower back. "Like this?" He turned, unabashed that his large cock was swelling and rising from his patch of dark hair.

The size of it chipped at her courage and she locked her knees to stop from turning and running. What was the point? He'd only chase her. She'd pushed him too far now.

A booming clap of thunder brought her back to her plan.

"On the bed," she ordered again as she reached for the belt that held her tunic close to her waist. As she slowly freed it, Haakon sat with his back straight against the carved, wooden headboard.

He looked so big and brooding, turned on and anticipatory. A sudden new thought popped into her mind: she hoped she would live up to his expectations. He'd been desiring her for weeks.

Could she do this?

Resisting the urge to break her eye contact with his, she tossed the belt aside. Next, she opened the buttons on her twill, woolen tunic, revealing the rise of her breasts poking up from the red binding she wore when riding.

He was utterly still, drinking her up, following her every move.

With the tunic gone, she pushed at her pants, stooping to remove her leather shoes.

When she straightened wearing nothing but her breast binding, Haakon swallowed noisily, his Adam's apple bobbing low and then his chest filling as he took a deep breath.

His attention went to the juncture of her thighs and he fisted the sheets.

"You are impatient, husband," she said, pushing away the thought that he was only just in control of his lust. It was like him grasping a hair to hold his weight, or standing on thin ice. It could easily snap and he'd be consumed by his passion.

"What hot-blooded man wouldn't be impatient?" He kind of grimaced and gritted his teeth. "You are a temptation too much to withstand."

She laughed softly and reached behind herself to undo her breast binding. "You are doing so well."

"Not for long." His cock bobbed and he reached for it, held it tight in his fist, and with his thumb toyed with the ring piercing at the end.

Summoning courage, Kenna walked forward, slowly, rolling her hips with each step. The way he was looking at her made her feel more beautiful than she ever had before, as though she really was, in this moment, the center of Haakon's world.

And for some reason, that added to the sense of power she had always stoked within herself. It felt good. *He* made her feel good.

"You want me to take this off?" she asked, loosening the binding.

"*Ja*. I want to see you naked, for the first time, like this in the light of the fire." He frowned and shook his head. "You are more beautiful than I could have ever imagined."

"You must have thought that to wish to marry me." She let the binding drop to the floor.

"*Ja*, but I'm sure many a man has had disappointment on his wedding night." Haakon's gaze slipped to her breasts.

Her nipples were tight and tingling.

"But not me," he murmured. "You were worth the wait." He released his cock and reached for her waist. "Come to me."

She allowed him to pull her onto the bed, then she sat astride his thighs, her hands on his shoulders and his erection between them.

"I want you more than I have ever wanted a woman," he murmured, looking up into her eyes.

"As it should be."

"And I will never want another." He held her right breast and brushed his thumb over her nipple. "Until the day I die and beyond, my body will only join with yours."

Heat spread from his touch, down to her belly, to her pussy. "Unless a beautiful woman rides into—"

"No!" He downturned his mouth. "Only you, my Valkyrie, my queen, my wife, that is my promise to you."

She leaned forward and brushed her lips over his. "But how can you be so sure? How were you so sure from the first moment?"

"I just knew," he whispered. "The gods had spoken, all of the gods, yours and mine. In that moment, new life came back to me and I saw your face I knew that I would always be bound to you." He paused and sat forward, crushing his chest to hers and cupping her face. "If I am a river. You are the sea I rush to. If I am the dawn, you are the birdsong I long for. If I were a scattering of stars, it would be you, the moon, I would long to be with."

"Haakon," she managed, hardly believing her ears. The wild monster she'd found on the beach wove words with skill and each one had sewn itself into her heart.

"I love you," he said. "Please, let me show you how much."

"Aye, aye, you should do that."

Chapter Twenty

HAAKON STUDIED HIS wife's flushed face. She'd never been more irresistible with her wide, desire-filled pupils and her lips still damp from his kiss.

"Tell me you want me," he murmured. "As a woman truly wants a man, not out of any sense of duty."

She hesitated and he could have kicked himself for asking the question. His cock was aching for her, his heart thudding with impatience. "Kenna, my love." He frowned.

"I want you," she said quietly, "but…but be gentle with me. And the ring on your… I—"

"If I hurt you, I would leave these lands with my head hanging in shame." He pulled her closer and kissed her, relieved when she slipped her tongue into his mouth and searched for his. The last thing he wanted was for her to be scared or hurt by him. He only wanted to make her feel good. So good. The best she'd ever felt.

She moaned softly and the sound went straight to his cock, filling it further when it was already so hard.

He wanted to touch her everywhere but didn't know where to start, so he slid his hands onto her slender shoulders and then down her lean back. Her skin was like a polished pebble and so warm and alive. She was delicate yet strong and her scent, lavender and the freshness of a spring morning, filled his nose.

His balls tightened and his cock demanded attention. "Kenna," he managed against her lips. "Sit on me. Take me."

"I…I don't know how." She pulled back and her eyes flashed with uncertainty. "And what if the ring comes off inside me?"

"It won't. I promise. And it's easy. Sit like this." He lifted her by her waist and positioned her pussy over his cock. "Are you wet for me?"

"I…I don't know." She pressed her lips together anxiously. "Is that important?"

He smiled at her. "It helps."

Leaning forward, he flicked his tongue over her sweet, little, pale nipple. It hardened instantly and she gripped his shoulders tighter.

She liked that. *Good.*

Switching to her other breast, he stroked down her flat belly and to her pubic hair. It was soft and warm and he slipped through it until he found her pussy.

"Oh!" she gasped, her eyes widening.

"Let me touch you," he said. "I will make this work for us."

She nodded and nibbled on her bottom lip.

Oh, in the name of all the gods, she was wet and hot and her soft, plump lips were the stuff his fantasies had been made of since the day he'd met her. "Kenna," he managed. "We will be perfect together."

He slipped into her entrance, her moisture coating his finger as he drove knuckle deep. Her tightness gripped him and her muscles fluttered around him.

Her lips parted and her head fell back a little as though lost to sensation.

"You are ready for a man," he said onto her jawline. "Ready for me."

She nodded and rose a little higher, as though suddenly unsure of his finger being inside her.

"Trust me," he said, his free hand spanning one side of her waist. "I will make it good for you." He slipped from her but kept his fingers on her pussy, exploring, searching, looking for the spot that would have her gasping.

There, he'd found it. Her sweet nub.

"You like that?" he murmured, kissing down her neck.

"Oh…oh…yes… I…"

"Shh, just feel." He rubbed it firmer in a small, circular motion.

After a few moments, she canted her hips, searching for more, and clasped her hands behind his neck. He could smell her arousal now and a drip of pre-cum had leaked from his slit.

"Oh, dear Lord," she gasped. "What are you doing…? I…"

"I'm getting you ready for me," he said. "Now it will not hurt. Your body is craving it, craving me."

"Aye. Aye." She nodded. "Haakon…I…"

He circled her waist and lifted her slight weight, once again so she was over his cock. "Now you can take me." In the name of all the gods, if she didn't, he would die of frustration, of pent-up energy and desire. He'd explode, he was sure of it.

"I just sit?"

"*Ja*, just sit." He gripped his cock, holding it steady for her. "Now."

Her damp entrance touched his cock tip and he groaned with longing as his ring pulled slightly on his slit—the longing was like a real, wild beast inside of him, clawing for penetration. "Relax, and take me," he managed, then he found her mouth; perhaps a kiss would help with his urge to throw her to the bed and bury hard and fast and take them both to breath-stealing orgasms.

Sinking onto him, she groaned low and guttural as his cock stretched her entrance.

Her gripping pussy almost had him cumming, but he fought it back and sat as still as he could while she took him another inch.

Then another inch.

Her heat surrounded him. Nothing else in the world existed. King Athol, Ravn, Odin himself could have marched into the room and Haakon would have ignored them.

"I don't know if—" She broke the kiss and pulled back, her fingers pincers on his shoulders.

"You can. We will fit perfectly together." He urged her down some more and her pussy took him.

She whimpered, but it wasn't a sound of pain—it was a sound of deep pleasure. Her head fell back and he cradled her skull, licking his way up her neck.

"Aye, aye, that is it…" she said, her voice strained as she seemed to suddenly give way to him. Taking him. Her ass cheeks landing on his thighs.

He moaned and clutched her to him, her breasts squashing against his chest. Finally. After all this time, he'd claimed his wife.

He let her adjust to his invasion then gripped her hips. "Move, like this," he whispered.

For a moment, she faltered, then with a little persuasion, she began to rock on him.

He closed his eyes and hissed in a breath. His sweet wife was going to be his undoing. He was at her mercy.

And then she found it. The exact movement she needed so her little nub crushed onto his body, stimulating it the way he'd been with his fingers.

"Oh! Haakon." She stared at him wide-eyed and repeated the movement. "I…I…"

"You understand now," he said. "How to find your pleasure."

She swallowed and nodded.

He cupped her right breast, tugging her nipple through a gap in his fingers. "And I promise not to find mine until you do." Oh, how he hoped he'd be able to keep that promise.

"It feels good," she said, rolling on and over him.

His cock was being massaged as she moved. The tug of her body on the ring stimulated him further.

"It feels *really* good," she gasped.

"It always will." He curled his toes and bent his knees, willing his body to obey. He was so close. His cock as hard as it ever got.

She moaned and buried her head in the groove of his neck and shoulder. She was riding him hard now, working her nub on him, her pussy full of him.

He clasped her ass, absorbing the thrusting of her small body on his.

"It's so much… It's…" Her fingernails dug into the flesh on his upper arms.

"Take your pleasure," he almost growled. "Now."

"Oh, oh, it's here." She flung back her head, her hip movements almost violent, and let out a wail of pleasure.

He joined her, crying out as his release blasted up his cock and he erupted inside of her.

Still, she went on, her pussy pulsing around his shaft and her body slick with sweat against his.

Everything about her was incredible. He'd never held such a creature in his arms, or been inside such a beautiful and giving woman.

Then she slumped against him, shaking, trembling, her pussy quivering and her breaths coming like small storms onto his hot skin.

"My love," he said, stroking her hair. "You are truly my wife now."

"Aye," she said, keeping her head buried in his neck. "I am."

"And I hope you are pleased with your husband's cock."

"Aye, I am." She giggled and lifted her head, looking into his eyes. "Thank you."

"For what?"

"For letting me be in control."

"You control my heart." He tipped his head and smiled. "You have turned it from a heavy, black stone into red flesh and blood that beats only for you."

Kenna studied Haakon's flaring nostrils, his lips shiny from their kisses. Perspiration sat on his forehead and over his top lip and his eyes glinted with satisfaction... No, it was more than that. It was male pride, she was sure of it.

"As mine beats only for you," she whispered, adjusting the leather strap his boar fang hung on.

"Do you mean that?"

"Aye, husband, I do."

"You have made me the happiest man in all of Lothlend." His eyes flashed with pleasure.

"You will be happier when you defeat King Athol."

"King who?" He laughed. "No one else exists for me, not tonight, not here. It is just you and me."

"And the owl." She nodded upward.

Haakon chuckled. "Oh, *ja*, him. He seems to like that spot and at least we know we'll not be bothered with mice."

His cock moved inside her, as though it had a life of its own.

"I don't want to move," he said. "Having you sitting on me, naked... That's where I want to stay."

The wind pressed extra hard against the side of the building and more thunder rumbled in the distance.

She slipped from him. The sweat on her back was cooling and she had to suppress a shiver.

He moaned in complaint but then reached for the furs and pulled them upward, over them both.

Kenna curled up on her side and Haakon scooped in behind her, his big body as warm as any fire.

Her pussy felt swollen and wet and her body heavy. The hunger that had been clawing at her had been satisfied and she sighed contentedly.

"Sleep," he murmured as he kissed her ear. "And know you are safe in my arms, my beautiful queen."

She sighed and seemed to sag into his embrace all the more and fall deeper into the bed. Sleep was encroaching fast, the sudden weariness like nothing she'd felt before.

Her thoughts began to scatter, mixing into a jumbled blur, and then she was dreaming. Soft, gentle dreams that were full of the images and sensations she'd just learned.

When Kenna woke the storm had passed. She knew this before she'd even opened her eyes, the stillness almost as loud as the thunder.

Behind her, Haakon kept her warm and his breaths were steady. A smile spread on her lips as the memories of the night before came flooding back.

She truly was his wife now, his queen. After all that worry, her protests, the anxious wondering, she'd lain with him, and to her surprise, enjoyed every moment of it.

She hoped it wouldn't be too long before they did it again.

His cock was nestled between her ass cheeks and she wriggled a little, feeling the hardness of the metal ring.

He moaned softly and his hold on her tightened.

And then she felt it, his cock growing. Almost magically, it stiffened against her, more and more, until it was totally solid.

"You woke me," he murmured against her ear.

"I am sorry. I will—"

She started to move, but he gripped her tighter.

"It is not just me you woke, but also my cock. And he's a demanding bugger in the morning."

Her heart rate, which had been slow, suddenly tripled. "But I...? Now?"

"Don't deny yourself this," he said, kissing her neck and sliding one hand to her breast. "Morning sex is one of life's greatest gifts."

Her pussy fluttered and she was aware that it was still a little damp.

"Like this." He used his legs to part hers and then his cock was there, probing at her, the ring cold and solid against her delicate flesh.

"Can we... I mean, does it work like this?"

"*Ja*, and I think you'll like it."

As he'd spoken, he'd found her entrance and pushed in.

She gripped his forearms and arched her back. He was so hot and hard and she wanted a repeat of the night before.

"Mmm, *ja*, like that," he said, sliding his touch from her breast to between her legs. "Open up and take me."

He entered her deeper, pushing determinedly but still gently.

Her pussy let him in, and his cock ring rubbed over places that had her closing her eyes and groaning at the new deep, dense sensation.

When he hit full depth, he stilled.

She pushed back onto him, wanting to work her hips the way she had the night before.

"Let me," he whispered as he found her nub. "I know what you need."

She groaned as he applied the perfect pressure over and over, rubbing, stimulating. Creating that need for more and more until she burst.

He was breathing hard and fast, his hips thrusting, and he had her body locked tightly to his.

Kenna closed her eyes, lost to him and what he was doing to her. Last night, she'd been in control. Now it was his turn.

And she trusted him. Totally.

"My beautiful viqueen," he murmured. "We will make such wonderful sons together."

"And daughters," she answered breathlessly. "Oh...don't stop."

Suddenly, he did just that. He pulled out and tipped her onto her back.

"Haakon!" She stared up at him. "What...?"

"Like this. I want to see your face." He settled between her legs and cupped her cheeks.

His weight was heavy on her, not too much, but enough to know he was still in control.

His cock found her entrance and she drew up her knees, bucking her hips. Greedy to feel him there again.

"Ah, *ja*..." he said, staring into her eyes and sinking deep. "Take me like you need me. Like you really need me."

"I *do* need you." She clasped his head, over his ears, the newly shaved skin smooth on her fingertips. "I need you to give me pleasure."

"That is the only thing that is going to happen." His body rocked over hers, rolling on her small, hard nub that was demanding attention.

"Oh...like that." She followed his movement, dancing beneath him for more. "Oh, Haakon, give it to me."

He gave it, driving into her, almost pulling out, then giving it to her again. Her heart beat wildly, her skin tingled, and the pressure in her pelvis was building. She stared into his eyes, lost to them, lost to him. It was as if she could see right into his soul and she was sure he could see into hers.

And what she saw was a man who was strong and determined, skilled and passionate. He was also loyal and brave and she knew, in that moment, that he'd always be there for her.

And she wanted to always be there for him. Give him heirs. Grow old together.

"My love...are you nearly there?" His brow was shiny with perspiration and the boar fang had caught between their chests.

"Aye...oh..." She pulled him in for a kiss and as their mouths met, her pleasure burst wildly from her pussy, spreading around her body. Shaking her, stealing her breath, pouring through her veins.

He cried out, the sound filling her mouth. She caught it and dragged her nails down his back to his ass, pulling him deeper as she canted her hips upward.

His release was hot and potent and for a moment, his gentleness slipped and he rammed in hard.

This just sent more pleasure racing around her body. She clung to him tighter, fearing she'd shatter if he didn't keep holding her together.

He broke the kiss. His eyes were glazed as he slowed and retook his weight on his arms.

"My love," she whispered breathlessly. "I am sure we have made a son this morning."

"It is my wish," he said, touching his lips to the tip of her nose. "But if we haven't, I will not complain, as we can keep trying."

Chapter Twenty-One

"I AM WORRIED about Astrid," Kenna said as she peeled the shell off a cooked egg. "It has been many days since we saw her and the storms have been coming one after another like a row of biting ants marching over the skies."

Haakon studied the frown line on his wife's brow. He hated to see her worried about anything. But this was one thing she didn't need to fret about. "Astrid can take care of herself."

"But this is a strange land."

"That is true." He sipped warm ale and glanced at their log basket. He'd have to restock later. "But it is a land that is not as harsh as where she grew up. That was very far north of here. And last winter, she took a coming-of-age walk and survived. More than that, she thrived, reported on her return that she'd enjoyed the solitude and had eaten well."

"'A coming-of-age walk'?" Kenna salted her egg then bit into it.

"*Ja*, straight after Yule, she headed for the mountains with only what she could carry in order to test her adult skills. And that winter..." He sighed. "The weather was truly Thor's plaything and he hammered and blew and brought down the snow so deep, it would cover the tallest man."

Her eyes widened. "I have never seen snow that deep. However did she survive?"

"With ancient knowledge and the guidance of the gods. And snow that deep, it is the way of the true north.

"Tell me more about the true north."

"The snow, it gathers on the mountains until it is so heavy, it falls down in one big blanket that pulls the trees from their roots with its force. It moves rocks, it carves new gullies, and the roar…" He shook his head. "It is as if the Ragnarök is upon us."

"Aye, Ragnarök, you have told me of this. When the great serpent spits its venom over everything, the wolves eat the sun and the moon, and then the earth and the gods battle with the fire giants and are defeated."

Haakon nodded, pleased that she remembered his saga.

"And if this is your story of how the world ends, Haakon, how do you tell it started?"

He leaned back in his chair, the new woolen cushion soft on his lower back. Their sex had been intense the night before, but he had a nice sense of satisfaction that had spread through his bones. "The great god Odin and his brothers created it."

"With what?"

"From the body of Ymir. From his blood, they made all the sea and the lakes. They used his flesh to create the earth we stand on. And his hair, they made the trees and all their leaves and branches." He leaned forward, enjoying her widening eyes. "And from his bones, the mountains were shaped. They made rocks and pebbles from his teeth and jaws."

"That is…quite the saga," she said.

"'Saga'?" He nodded slowly. For him, it was more than a saga, it was a truth. Yet his wife knew not of it and now he was supposed to understand her belief and believe less of his. He was trying, but it was hard to let go of a lifetime of certainty in his gods and let a new one in. Luckily, Kenna understood his swinging between, as he learned her way and the ways of his new people.

"So how do you think it was made?" he asked. "What does the church say?"

She frowned a little and looked at the cross he'd made her. She'd set it on the table beside the bed.

"Kenna?"

"It was made in six days by God Himself. He spoke aloud to bring order to the chaos that was the sun, the stars, and the moon and brought all living things into existence."

Haakon tipped his head, intrigued to hear a new saga.

She waved her hand in the air, warming to her story. "The fact that He created it so quickly proves His almighty power. And He named everything, the deer, the bee, the river, and the shells. It is all His will."

"And people? He made people too?"

"Of course. In the Garden of Eden."

"'The Garden of Eden'?"

"Aye." She smiled. "And He created Adam in the form of Himself and Eve from Adam's rib."

"Ah, the way Ymir's body parts created things. So did Adam's rib."

"A little like that, I suppose." She smiled. "Eden is a beautiful garden that is fruitful and bathed in sunshine all year round. The streams flow pure and the moss is the softest bed you could ever imagine."

"I should like to go to this place." Haakon sat forward, excited at the thought of this garden. "And meet Adam and Eve."

She laughed softly and brushed the eggshells into a wastebasket. "You cannot go there now, or meet Adam and Eve."

"Why not? We can build a bigger boat if necessary. I am capable of many days riding and walking."

"But they are not here now. Not anywhere."

"How do you know?"

"It is the teachings of the Bible." She stood and came to him, sat on his lap, and wrapped her arms around his neck. "Adam and Eve disobeyed God by eating the one fruit he told them not to. They sinned and in turn created evil in all people."

"But what fruit was it?" This was a very strange story, but he was happy to listen to all the details now that she was in his arms. "How can fruit be so bad?"

"It was an apple on the tree of knowledge, good and evil. And the serpent told them—"

"Ah, there is a serpent in your story too."

She smiled. "The serpent told them to eat it, for why should they not have knowledge too? And it was Eve who took it, ate it. She gave some to Adam."

"And then what happened?" He stroked his hand down her slender back, enjoying the fact that he knew how it felt to touch her naked body now.

"God was angry. They had disobeyed Him when He'd given them everything. He sent them out of the Garden of Eden with their hearts full of shame and regret and we have been paying the price ever since."

"'Paying the price'?"

"Aye." She stroked her finger down his cheek as if still learning his face. "We suffer, we know pain, we have the torment of loss and grief. If Eve had never picked that apple—"

"You truly believe that you live a hard life because of Eve?"

"Aye."

"But what about when there is a good harvest and the sun shines and new babes are born with life in their lungs? That is not hardship."

"I agree. God is benevolent, He is merciful and kind, not like your Thor, who seems to be constantly angry and Odin, who is all-seeing through his ravens."

"It is true my gods, or the gods of my people, for I am Christian now, are keen to make themselves known."

"I am interested in your gods." She brushed her lips over his. "And although you now worship the one true God, I enjoy your sagas about them."

"You are also benevolent."

"I have come to think of your gods differently. My mother helped me with that."

"Your mother?" Haakon raised his eyebrows. "She barely says a word to me. What does she say to you?"

Kenna chuckled. "Things that should stay between a mother and daughter, but what I will tell you is…"

"What?" He pulled her nearer, enjoying her slight weight on his lap.

"It was she who opened my eyes to the fact that I was neglecting my wifely duties."

"Ah, so I should thank her." His heart squeezed at the memory of watching Kenna strip off her clothes that first time as she'd stood by the fire. She'd been exquisite. Every curve and slope, each hair and delicate tremble was imprinted on his memory.

She slanted her head and kissed him, her tongue probing for his.

He groaned and clasped her tighter. In his wildest dreams, in his most fevered hopes, he'd never dared imagine she'd be this responsive, this open for him.

"Haakon!" Gunner's voice.

"Go away," Haakon called. He kissed down his wife's neck as he cradled the back of his head.

"King Haakon!" Orm's voice this time, high and singsong, as if mocking.

"I said, *get out of here!*" Haakon bellowed.

"No," Orm shouted. "We have work to do."

"We'll do it later."

"The men are assembled, and there is a reprieve between storms," Gunner said from behind the curtained doorway.

"The men?" Haakon ran his hand to Kenna's breast and squeezed it over her gown. He didn't want to go anywhere.

"The men, the villagers, they are ready with pikes and newly made shields awaiting your instruction," Orm said, banging on the curtain so it punched inward. "So put your bride down, free up your hands from her breast, tell your cock to stop thinking of her pussy, and train yourself an army to be proud of."

"Of all the…" Haakon frowned, frustration a coiled snake within him. "Bad timing." His cock was at half-mast and getting naked had been at the forefront of his mind.

"Husband," Kenna said. "It will be nightfall again soon enough and I will be waiting for you."

"That pleases me," he said. "But I need you with me. A queen must be able to defend herself."

"I can—"

"It is true you have skills, but now, my adorable wife, you must learn Viking skills, for our enemies are many and one day soon, King Athol will ride up to our fort."

"You are right." She slipped from his lap and he felt the loss as much as if he'd had an arm chopped off. "I must hone my fighting skills."

The determined glint in her eyes distracted him from the discomfort in his pants and he stood. How lucky he was to have a wife who was as eager to storm the battlefield as she was to jump into their bed.

A FEW MINUTES later, Haakon stood on the snowy earth outside the fort gates and surveyed the motley crew before him. They were farmers, hunters, a few fishermen along with the ironsmith, cobbler, and carpenter. Bryce was there, but still no Hamish, and a handful of strong, young women held their new shields defiantly, as if waiting to be sent away and argue the point about being allowed to fight.

"The storms have passed," Haakon bellowed, walking up and down the quiet line. "Which means our lessons in combat will begin. I see some of you have crossbows. This is good and also essential to our shield wall."

"What is a shield wall?" Noah asked from where he stood bent over his cane.

"It is a tactic that has proven itself over and over." Haakon gestured to half the men and then pointed to the left. "You, that way. Ten crossbows too."

There was a shuffle around.

"Now we need three rows with the crossbows at the back."

Another shuffle.

"And now, everyone, hold up your shields so that they are overlapping, an impenetrable wall."

A clack and clatter of wood.

"That's it good." Haakon clapped and pointed to his right. "Now imagine these men are King Athol and his tax-collector warriors. When we refuse to pay they will attack, but if we are in a shield wall..." He gestured to the solid mass of shields. "Their arrows cannot penetrate, and when they have fired and are reloading our men can fire arrows with the protection of the wall. Any survivors who rush at us will be blocked by our shields, but the beauty of it is our swords and daggers can still jab. We will take them out one by one yet all the time have the protection of our shields."

"And if the shield wall breaks?" Bryce asked, hands on his hips. "If some of our men are killed?"

Haakon was irritated just by Bryce's voice. It did things to his bile and blood.

"It inevitably will," he said.

"And then what?" Anna, the carpenter's daughter, asked. Her hair was tucked under a scarf and her pink cheeks rounded, like crab apples.

"That is when we fight. That is when..." Haakon raised his voice. "We destroy the enemy. The men who wish us to pay for what is rightfully ours, to use what God gave to us." He banged his hand on his chest. "That will never happen again. Now that I am king, we will find justice, even if it means a fight."

"And if King Athol disputes your claim to a crown..." Bryce stepped forward. "Then what?"

"I am expecting him to." Haakon marched up to meet Bryce. "Which is why we are preparing."

"And if he brings a large army? What if word has gotten out that we are to fight and he comes in the night and slays us all?"

"We will ensure our watchmen are alert and we sleep with our swords." Haakon clicked his tongue on the roof of his mouth. "It's an easy solution."

Bryce was quiet for a moment, his eye contact unwavering with Haakon's. That also irritated Haakon.

"Husband." Kenna was at his side, her hand on his arm. "Bryce is simply playing devil's advocate. Pointing out all the worst scenarios."

"He is a pessimist."

"I am not," Bryce said. "Because the worst has already happened." He tipped his left eyebrow and looked between Haakon and Kenna. He kept his attention firmly on her.

"And that is?" Haakon growled.

"You married her."

"And that is a problem for you?" Haakon stepped forward, so close to Bryce that their chests were touching.

"Aye, it is." Bryce tipped his chin to look up at Haakon. "You can't just march in and take another man's woman."

"I was never your woman, Bryce," Kenna said calmly.

"You would have been, eventually."

Haakon lowered his face and snarled. "The gods made Kenna *my* destiny, not yours. You need to accept that and get out of my way."

"Gods, see? You got her by trickery. You do not believe in the one true God."

Anger was hot and red and flowing through Haakon's veins. "As you could not learn all about my gods in a matter of weeks, I cannot learn all about yours, but I am learning and seeing the light."

"He is," Kenna said, seemingly trying to slot herself between him and Bryce. "Please, Bryce, step away."

"*Ja*, get out of my way," Haakon snapped. "Before I am forced to challenge you to the death."

"I would rather die than stay here and watch Kenna be raped by you, carry your heathen children, and—"

Haakon's anger erupted and he shoved at Bryce, hard, and felt a keen sense of satisfaction when the other man reeled backward and staggered to stay upright.

"You want to know why Hamish is gone, Kenna?" Bryce said breathlessly as he straightened. "Because he feels the same as me. He can't live here with you betrothed to this monster."

"That is not why Hamish has left," Kenna said, emotion making her voice thick. "It isn't."

"I will warn you to close your mouth," Haakon said, his hand automatically going to the leather-wrapped handle of his sword. "Because I could strike you down with one slice of my weapon."

"I would like to see you try." Bryce raised his sword. "For do not underestimate me or my skills."

"Please, no." Kenna rushed between the two men, her hood falling and her hair whisking up in the wind. At that moment, a streak of sunlight burst through the clouds and landed where she stood.

Haakon's breath caught in his throat. She was so beautiful, truly a Valkyrie, even if she didn't know it yet. He'd do anything for her.

"Please, Haakon, my love. Please don't hurt my friend."

"It is I who will hurt him," Bryce snarled behind her.

She spun to face Bryce. "This is how it is now. I am your queen and Haakon is your king *and* he is my husband, you must accept that."

"How can I ever accept it?" Bryce's eyes narrowed and his jaw tightened. "When I have loved you from the moment I could walk and talk."

Kenna stilled, her shoulders pushed down and her hands balled into fists.

Out of the corner of his eye, Haakon could see Orm grinning and hopping from one foot to the other. He was enjoying the show.

"And I love you, Bryce," Kenna said.

Haakon bristled and his legs throbbed with the need to spring into action—spring on Bryce and unleash his anger.

"But not as I ever would love a husband," Kenna went on. "And if you accept that, you will marry another and be happy."

Bryce tipped his chin and his eyes glistened.

Kenna turned to Haakon, her face aglow with emotion. "Please, let this go." She stepped up to him and curled her hand over his, which was wrapped around his sword handle. "When the heart is hurt it is a burden to bear. Bryce is carrying that burden right now."

"It is a burden, a burden you must bear." Orm was beside Bryce. He slapped him on the shoulder and laughed. "Carry your burden."

"Fuck off," Bryce muttered as he shrugged.

"I will not hurt him," Haakon said. "Because you have asked me not to and I will do anything for you, my viqueen."

She smiled, and Haakon knew in that moment that not only was he in love with his wife, he was also wrapped around her little finger, just as had been predicted.

Chapter Twenty-Two

KENNA BLEW OUT a breath and picked up a shield and long dagger. She stood beside Anna, ready to learn. The snow beneath them had been trampled and mixed with the earth. Patches of mud were forming.

The clouds broke apart, revealing the milky blue of a winter sky and Haakon, Gunner, Orm, Knud, and Ivar set about sharing their skills of the sword and shield with the men and women of Tillicoulty.

This was to be a daily occurrence from this point on, Haakon had declared. When chores were complete, honing warrior skills must be the priority, especially in winter months when there was less to do in the fields.

"Your husband is proving to be a fine man," Olaf said with an approving nod when Kenna took a rest beside him.

"Which is more than I thought I'd ever agree with when he marched into our village," Kenna replied.

"Does he treat you well?" Noah asked. "As a husband."

"He doesn't beat me." She raised her eyebrows at her father. "If that is what you are asking."

"If he beat you, I would dust off my sword and slay him down." Noah grimaced. "I may be old, but I would always defend and protect you, even from a Norse king. Even if it meant my certain death."

"I know, Father." She smiled and kissed his cheek. "But there is no need. He treats me as if I am one of his goddesses. Whatever I want, he provides. At all times, he looks to see how he can make me more comfortable, happier, and…"

"And?" Olaf asked, leaning in, curiosity sparkling in his old eyes.

"He treats me as an equal. He takes notice of what I say, seeks my counsel on matters, and appreciates my skills."

"Their women are different to ours. Look at his sister." Noah nodded thoughtfully. "How she was. How she acted as though she were invincible, immortal, even."

"And I like that they treat women differently," Kenna said. "I am more to my husband than a broodmare. I am my own person."

Noah nodded slowly and bit on his bottom lip.

"It is unusual, indeed," Olaf said. "And we must accept that it is God's will that he came upon our shores."

"God works in mysterious ways. Ways we can never hope to understand," Kenna said with a smile. "Now if you'll excuse me, I'm going to change from these clothes. Rolling in the dirt and dodging Orm's sword has rendered me filthy."

"I'm glad that was a wooden sword," Noah said. "He didn't go easy on you."

"I wouldn't want him to." Kenna glanced at where Orm was now teaching Caitlin, a curly-haired, freckled fisherman's daughter, how to swing her sword to block his. "For we all need to be ready. When we are attacked everyone will have a role to play."

"Aye, it is a *when*, not an *if*." Noah sighed. "King Athol will be most aggrieved not to receive taxes from us. It is how it has always been."

"How it has always been has changed," Kenna said. "Now the Vikings are here."

Kenna walked back under the watchtower and was greeted by Lass. She stroked her head and tickled her chin. "Go to Mother," she said. "I hear she is cooking chicken."

Lass reacted to the word *chicken* as she always did, her ears pricking up and her tongue coming out.

"Go," Kenna said with a laugh. "And find yourself some food."

Lass barked once then ran off in the direction of what used to be Kenna's home.

Now the Great House was where she lived and she was glad for it. Her legs were weary and her hair sticky with mud. She pulled a dry leaf from her bangs as she approached. The weak sun had warmed her shoulders, but not enough to warm her bones, and a sudden longing to bathe came over her.

Aye, she'd warm some water over the fire and use the large barrel Haakon had sawed in half to bathe in. He bathed often, changed his clothes regularly, and often smelled of his chestnut soap. He'd also made her a skin moisturizer out of wool-fat, butter, and rosemary oil. It smelled divine and she was keen to use it again.

Her bedchamber was quiet and the fire had nearly burnt out. Quickly, she stoked it then put a large pail of water over the growing flames.

She glanced at the corner. The owl was asleep. A small fluffy ball hunched in the shadows. He was a sign of good fortune, she was sure of it, watching over them and guiding prosperity their way.

After dragging the half-barrel before the fire, she stripped off her clothes. They'd need a good wash. Or perhaps she'd put them aside ready for tomorrow's training; they would only get dirty again.

As the water heated, she poured ale and took a sip. It slipped down her gullet and she traced her naked flesh with the tip of her finger. The cool air had tightened her nipples and she thought of how Haakon suckled them into his mouth when they lay together, how he licked and flicked them and had her moaning for more.

Never in all her life had she expected her wifely duties to be so thrilling, so all-consuming. Never would she have thought she'd be so satisfied after taking her husband's cock. It was a wonderful, complete feeling that went to every corner of her body. A far cry from the pain and humiliation she'd been expecting.

Were all men as skilled as Haakon when it came to bedding or was it just her husband? If the latter, she was very lucky.

She poured the steaming water into the barrel and put more on to heat. She then added a few drops of the slick rosemary oil. It beaded on the surface and she stirred it to dissipate the rich, aromatic scent.

Had her mother had the same experience with her father? Kenna couldn't imagine it. Did Hamish know it would be like this when he took a wife? Would he know what to do by instinct?

And would Bryce have given her the same breath-stealing climaxes if she'd eventually taken him as her husband?

She didn't think so.

Eventually, the barrel was over half full with warm, steaming water. Outside, a skein of geese flew overhead, honking as they went, announcing the daylight hours were drawing to an end.

She dipped her toe into the hot water, paused for a moment to ensure it wouldn't scald her, then gingerly stepped in. With her hands on the sides of the barrel, she sat, her eyes on the flames dancing in the grate.

How decadent it was to bathe like this. In the summer, she and her mother would go to the stream once a week, and in the winter, more often than not, it was a quick splash with a bowl of water.

But this...this Viking way of bathing was luxurious.

Once seated, she slowly scooted down, letting the water seep around her, into her, and up her back. She half-lay, half-sat, her nipples peeking from the water.

"Ah, this is a gift from God," she murmured as she closed her eyes. The heat penetrated right to her core, the water a balm on her aching muscles.

"No, it is a gift from me."

"What? I..." She opened her eyes.

Haakon stood in the doorway, his shoulders just about touching each side and his head slightly ducked.

"The bathing barrel," he said, stepping into the room. "I knew you would like it."

"I thought you had it made for yourself."

"What's mine is yours." He shrugged off his fur and tossed it over a chair. "You can have anything of mine you desire."

"You have already given me more than I ever thought you could."

"'Could' or 'would'?" He walked to the table and took a drink of ale.

"Could." She studied the way his inked throat moved as he drank.

He didn't reply. Instead, he rolled up his right sleeve and came and knelt by the barrel. "Do you have it nice and hot?"

"Aye."

He dipped his hand in. "Mm, it is a good way to warm up after a day on a battlefield."

"Do you think the village men will be able to defend Tillicoulty?"

"*Ja*, they are strong and determined. With practice, they will become warriors to be proud of."

"I hope so."

"They will. They have the best teacher." He shrugged.

She raised her eyebrows. "One thing I worry about is your lack of modesty, husband of mine."

He laughed softly. "Oh, I know I am good at everything I put my mind to." He ran his hand through the water, creating soft ripples.

He had a streak of mud on his right cheek and his nose was a little red from the cold day. He was watching her as intensely as she was looking at him.

His knuckles brushed her hip and then the outer edge of her thigh.

She hitched in a breath, her nipples poking further from the water.

He stroked down to her ankle then up again, over the curve of her hip to her waist and then over her belly.

Everywhere he touched left a heated trail of desire.

"Your wet skin is making me hard," he murmured. "You are like silk." His attention slipped to her pinched nipples. "You are like the mermaid on the famed mermaid axe."

"'Mermaid axe'?" she whispered.

He smiled, tension from his features slipping. "Legend has it that Bjorn the Bold was seafaring one day and—"

"Who is he? An ancestor of yours?"

"My father says that he is." He tipped his head and continued. "Bjorn came across a group of mermaids trapped upon the rocks. They were being attacked by a terrible serpent. He came to their rescue, slaying the serpent and clearing their way back to the ocean. The mermaids were so grateful, they gifted Bjorn an axe, the handle shaped as a beautiful woman with a fish tail and the blade magically infused with materials from land and sea, meaning it would never need to be sharpened."

"What an incredible axe, and Bjorn sounds like a compassionate man to have saved them."

"He was." Haakon skimmed his fingertips over her nipples, the water gently splashing. "He was valiant and skilled and—"

"And…?"

"And legend has it he had five wives and over twenty children."

Her eyes widened. "That is a lot of wives."

"You should also know…" he said softly as he ran his fingertips back under the water and to her navel. "That I only ever wish to have one wife."

She trembled as he dipped his fingers lower, toward the juncture of her thighs. Small ripples tapped over the surface of the water and she curled her toes.

"One wife whom I can kiss and touch and pleasure," Haakon said softly. "One wife for whom I will forsake all others."

He slipped his fingertip between her legs, smoothing over her soft, wet flesh.

"Oh…but…" Her mouth fell open. What was he expecting of her? Shouldn't they go to the bed?

"Shh." He smiled. "I want to touch you. I want to watch you."

"'Watch' me?"

"I want to watch you find pleasure." He swirled his fingertip over her nub.

She tensed. "Oh…"

"It's just here you like it, *ja*?"

She bit on her bottom lip and nodded. Her pussy tensed and her heart rate picked up as she parted her thighs.

"And there is no rush. We have all night." He swirled lazily. "You should relax and know that I am enjoying this even more than you are."

"Haakon," she gasped. "Surely, this is wrong in the eyes of—"

"How can it be wrong? We are married." He slipped lower and curled the tips of his fingers into her pliant, wet entrance. "And I'm sure Adam and Eve spent many days naked and seeking pleasure."

"Oh…but you can't say things like that…and…oh…Haakon." She closed her eyes, thoughts of Bible stories evaporating. "Aye, just there…oh…"

He'd entered her with two fingers and the heel of his hand had caught over her bud.

"Like this?" He rocked his hand, fingering her and stimulating her nub. "Is that where you need it?"

"Aye." She groaned, let her head fall back, and gripped the side of the bath.

"Think only of my touch," he murmured, still working her. "Nothing else exists."

She rocked gently with his movements. The pressure in her pussy was growing and she let her legs fall open until her knees touched the barrel.

His hand was hard on her, but not hard enough, and after a few minutes, she reached down and gripped his solid forearm.

"You want more?"

She opened her eyes and nodded.

The right side of his mouth tipped into a smile and a tendon flexed in his cheek. His eyes glinted with the light of the fire's reflection on the water.

"I did promise to give you everything I could." He added another finger into her pussy and pressed firmer on her nub.

"Oh…please…" She gripped him tighter. "Give it to me."

He moved into her again, over her, crushing her bud.

She whimpered in pleasure, the seeds of her climax now having come to life and growing strong. "Don't stop."

"Not until you tell me to." He stared into her eyes. "Not until you tell me."

She lifted her hips, mimicking the way she rubbed against him when his cock was deep inside of her. It was good with his hand, his fingers. Soon, she'd reach that pinnacle of pleasure.

Water splashed over the bath, her back arched, and her nipples were as tight pebbles. She'd given up on any type of composure or control of her facial expressions. The need for orgasm had her in its grip. She was greedy for it.

"Fuck, you're beautiful," he said. "Cum for me like this. I want to see and feel you cum."

"I am…oh… Haakon…I…" She had no breath left to speak with. It was trapped in her lungs like a great, big ball of pressure. The erotic explosion was about to detonate and there was nothing that could stop it.

She pushed up her hips and cried out, a great, long wail of sound that matched the intense push of release that jerked her body almost from the water.

Haakon stayed with her, pumping his fingers into her, bashing up against her nub even, as she bucked and writhed as though possessed by some demon.

She cried out again and curled forward, opening her eyes. She could make out the fuzzy image of his wrist between her legs, his movements agitating the surface of the water.

"Oh…it's so much…" Her pussy was gripping his fingers as though it had a life of its own. Hard, little spasms that pulsed through her body and tightened all of her muscles.

"You are so giving and beautiful," he said hoarsely as he finally slowed. "And so responsive to my touch."

"It's…hard not…to be responsive." She was battling for breath. "When you do that."

He smiled, a big, wide grin that balled his cheeks. "I could touch you like this forever."

She reached for him, cupped his face, and kissed him. Her heart was beating wildly, a drum beat in her ears, and she was trembling as bliss winged through her veins.

How lucky she was that her husband was an ancestor of Bjorn the Bold and so very skilled at pleasing his woman.

Chapter Twenty-Three

HAAKON WAS WARM. The heat of the water and the flush on his wife's cheeks had heated his blood and stirred his desires.

He lifted his hand from the water and dragged off his tunic, tossing it aside.

Her attention drifted down his naked torso and he saw the approval in her eyes. It was a far cry from the disdain and fear he'd seen at the beginning of their marriage. Now she looked at him with almost as much passion as when he looked at her.

"Here," he said, passing her a woolen blanket. "For when you are ready to get out. Do you need more hot water?"

She shook her head and held his eye contact.

"Are you sure?"

"I have finished bathing." She smiled, just a little, and it was such a mischievous, confidant tilt of her lips that his cock swelled a bit more.

And then she unfolded and stood up in the tub. Water ran down her body, over the slope of her breasts, the dip of her waist, and dripped from her fingers. Her pale skin was perfect and smooth and shone like a dew-coated meadow. Her nipples were tight beads and her bush of hair was wet against her body.

He licked his lips as another rush of heat went to his groin and his cock strained against his pants. He was one lucky Viking. His wife was more beautiful than he deserved, he knew that. She was a goddess, an image carved by the gods, and she had found him, come to him, and now she would be his for all eternity.

"Haakon," she said, holding out her hand.

He took it and held her steady while she stepped from the tub. The scent of rosemary filtered up his nose and he knew it would become one of his new favorite scents.

"You seem a wee bit… trance-like?" she said, standing before him, proud now, not bashful. The strands of her hair were damp and clinging to her shoulders in thick curls.

"You enchant me so." He reached out and touched her right nipple.

It responded immediately, as did she with a small intake of breath.

"From the first moment I saw you," he said, "my body has longed for yours."

"As it does now." She hadn't said it as a question.

He bit on his bottom lip and nodded, wondering if she'd allow him to throw her to the bed and show her just how hard he was for her…how much he needed her.

"So let me see," she said with a tip of her head.

"'See'?"

"Aye, your cock. I want to see it…properly."

"You have seen it."

"Are you saying I can't? When you look at me as though I am some delicious morsel you are desperate to taste?"

His stomach clenched and he licked his lips again. That was exactly how he was looking at her. He wanted to taste her all over and have her screaming his name in pleasure. He'd replace those drips of water lacing her skin with a sheen of sex sweat.

"Husband?" She raised her eyebrows at him and placed her hands on her hips.

"*Ja?*" He cleared his throat.

"I want to see your cock."

She nodded at his groin and his cock twitched with anticipation.

"You want to…"

"Take off your pants," she said, reaching for the blanket and squeezing out the ends of her hair with it. "Show me."

He toed off his boots then undid the belt at his waist. His balls were tight and a hunger was growing in him. One that only his wife could satisfy. "You want to see my cock?"

"I want to see all of you. If you are truly mine, that is."

"I am yours from this day until my last breath and then beyond."

She stepped up closer and a shadow caressed half of her face. "That pleases me."

His heart was thumping and he pushed at his pants, letting them fall down his legs before kicking them away. His cock was throbbing with want. When had a woman ever had him so riled up before?

Never.

"Is it painful?" she asked. "Your cock?"

"It aches for you."

She nodded and stepped around him, surveying his body as one might a horse before a long journey. Checking for health, stamina, and strength.

"How did you get this?"

A fluttering sensation on the scar at the back of his thigh.

"A battle with my brother Ravn?"

"Your brother did this?" Shock hung in her voice.

He huffed. "No, we were fighting together, south of Drangar. A berserker showed up. Crazed and feral. I got too close."

"A berserker?"

"Aye, mercenary fighters. They feast on amanita before battle to give them courage and energy. They are much feared because they fear nothing."

"What happened to this...berserker?" Her voice was as soft as the glow of the candles. Her touch on his leg so delicate, it could have been butterfly wings.

He closed his eyes and spoke again. "My brother killed him."

"Ravn?"

"*Ja*, and not a second too soon. One more blow of his sword and I would have lost my guts."

"That is horrible." She paused. "And good of Ravn."

"We fought many battles together. We always had each other's back."

"Yet now you have quarreled so." She ran her hand upward, tracing the serpent that curved in a big 's' around his spine.

Haakon opened his eyes again and stared at the flames. "He believed himself better than me, more worthy of the crown. There was not enough room in Drangar for us both."

She tickled a circle at the base of his neck. "And so you came here. To my lands."

She was in front of him again, her chin tilted and her eyes ablaze.

"It was my destiny," he whispered. "*You* were my destiny."

She bit on her bottom lip and as she did so, she took his cock into her hand.

A breath stuttered from his lungs and he looked down. Her small hand on his big cock was one of the most erotic sights he'd ever seen.

"I like your ring now," she whispered as she rolled over it with her fingertips. "At first, it scared me, but now…now it's part of you."

"I am glad that you have come to accept me…and it."

"Mmm." She pulled on his cock, slowly, root to tip, and with her free hand, she cupped his balls.

"In the name of all the gods in…oh…fuck…" Haakon locked his knees to stop himself from swaying. "You will ruin me, woman."

"Maybe that is my plan."

He cupped her face. "Ruin me. Wreck me. I am at your mercy."

"Do you mean that?"

"*Ja*." He groaned as she ran her tight fist up and down his cock again.

"I think I need a closer look," she said, sinking to her knees.

"Oh, fuck..." Haakon said, watching his naked wife fold before him. It was a sight he'd longed to see since the moment he'd decided she would be his, but there'd been times he'd never thought he would. Yet now...

"It is silver?"

"Ja." His belly was tight and his butt cheeks clenched. "It was a coin, melted down...shaped into a...oh...fuck."

She was gently tugging his ring, pulling at his slit. It sent a new wave of lust through his body.

"That..." he managed. "Feels so good when you do it."

"I want to make you feel good. I feel I should return the favor."

"Return away." He ran his hands into her hair. "And if you want to lick it..."

"Lick it?" She looked up at him. The shadows of her eyelashes casted on her cheeks.

"Do whatever you want with me."

He closed his eyes and willed himself not to cum right there and then.

And then the wet heat of her tongue spread over his slit, rimming his glans, exploring, tasting...caressing.

Again, he locked his legs. He dropped his head back and moaned. Her slow, delicate touch was as potent as any wild fucking could be.

"You like that?" she whispered.

"More than I could ever tell you." His fingers tightened in her hair. "Can you... Will you...?"

"What?"

"Take my cock... into your mouth."

She didn't answer with words, she answered by doing it. The dampness of her mouth slid around his cock, her taut lips replacing her hand as she let him slide over the soft blanket of her tongue.

The longed-for sensation was almost Haakon's undoing. He very nearly unraveled, let go of all self-control, and shoved deep, cumming as he did so.

But if he did that, she'd likely never suck his cock again and he wanted a lifetime of it.

So he summoned his willpower, every last shred of it, and held as still as he could.

She bobbed forward, and he was aware of the back of her throat on his ring.

He let out a deep, rumbling groan and tightened his fingers in her hair as she began to pull back up.

Still, she rolled his balls, and when she breathed gently on his saliva-coated cock tip, he had to lock his knees and his spine.

"Oh…don't stop," he said, moving his hips toward her again. "That feels so good."

She took him into her mouth again, gaining in confidence, and he slid happily to the back of her throat. Soon, she had her rhythm, in and out, her tongue fondling him and her fingers exploring.

He closed his eyes and lifted his face to the ceiling. The effort of not cumming was almost too much to bear. But it was the sweetest torture he could imagine.

"My love," he gasped. "I will release my seed…in your mouth…if you…"

He couldn't finish the sentence. He was there; his orgasm had him in its clutches. The back of her throat tugged his cock and he came. A big rush of release that tore a cry from his lungs. He gripped her head, stilling as another burst of bliss burst from him.

And another.

"Oh…fuck!" He pulled out, his balls throbbing and his cock hot and pulsing. "My love."

He dropped to his knees before her, still cradling her face. "I am sorry… I… So sorry. I just couldn't…"

Her eyes were glassy and her lips puffy. She licked them and stared into his eyes. "Why are you sorry?"

"I was rough... I didn't want to hurt you. And I—"

"You didn't hurt me." She frowned and pressed her palm over his thudding heart. "And I know you would have stopped if I'd needed you to."

"*Ja*, I would have." He touched his nose to hers. "Are you sure? I would hate myself..."

"Haakon. I wanted to take you in my mouth and I did. And from what I can tell, you enjoyed it."

He was still breathless. "I did. It was... You are...incredible."

"So I can do it again?"

"Whenever you want. Just say the word. No matter what we are doing, mid-fucking-battle, just say and...*ja*, you can do it. I will never complain."

She laughed softly. "That's good to hear."

"I'm under your spell." He swept his lips over hers. "Who would have thought I, King Haakon Rhalson, could be brought to his knees by a woman?"

"Ah, but I am not *any* woman. I am Queen Kenna of Tillicoulty."

"And a fine queen you are too."

She bit on her bottom lip.

"What worries you?" he asked.

"For a beautiful moment, I forgot about the threat of King Athol. But now...now I worry about him seeking us out. What he will do."

Haakon hated to see worry in her eyes. "Do not fear, and do not concern yourself. That is my job for I am king. I will worry for us both...for the village."

"I cannot help it."

He touched his lips to hers. "Maybe he won't come."

"He will. I know he will." Her jaw tensed. "It is his way."

"My love." He touched her cheek. "Know this truth: when he comes, we will be ready, and we will be victorious. We have the gods on our side."

"And he believes he has the one true God, which makes him think he'll win. That emboldens him further."

Haakon raised his eyebrows at her. "Which gods do you believe will be on our side?"

She sighed and slid her fingers over his ear and down his neck, her touch leaving a trail of heated sensation. "I believe that the more gods we have on our side, the better. Thor, Freya, Odin, and the Heavenly Father—let us have them all, for we will need them on the awful day King Athol shows his face."

"Haakon! Haakon! Where are you?"

"That is Orm again," Haakon said, snapping back and reaching for the blanket. "Cover yourself." The last thing he wanted was for his brother, or any other man, to see his wife naked. Her flesh was for his eyes only.

"King Haakon! We must speak with you at once," Orm shouted, his voice getting louder now. "It is urgent."

Kenna dashed into the shadows with the blanket wrapped around herself. "He's here," she said with wide eyes and her skin paling. "I know it."

"Who is here?"

"King Athol!"

"He's taking his last breaths if he is," Haakon muttered and grabbed his clothes.

"Where are you?" Gunner's voice.

"What do you both want?" Haakon stepped into his pants and dragged them up, securing them at the waist. He turned to Kenna. "Wait here."

Quickly, he slipped from the bedchamber, ensuring the curtain was properly closed.

Orm and Gunner were storming toward him.

"What is it?" he asked.

"It is our sister, Astrid," Orm said, coming to a halt.

"And the queen's brother, Hamish," Gunner added.

"Is she well?" Haakon asked. She was a skilled fighter and could survive, but that hadn't stopped him worrying.

"Yes, she looks well." Gunner gestured wildly with his hands. "Or at least I think so."

A knot of tension eased in Haakon's shoulder. "And Hamish?"

"Yes. Yes."

"So why disturb me when I am with the queen?" Haakon set his hands on his hips.

"This is not about them, Astrid and Hamish. This is about what they've seen. What knowledge they come with."

Haakon's belly squeezed with a new sense of unease. Had his wife sensed this moment was knocking at their door? Was that why King Athol had been on their minds...? He was here?

"You must come quickly and hear what they have to say." Gunner gestured to the door. "We have no time to waste. Hurry."

"Yes. Yes." Haakon nodded.

Gunner took off at a run, gripping the doorframe as he rounded it.

"Brother!" Orm flapped his arms like a frightened bird. "Come now."

"I will, I will. One moment." He flicked his hand, dismissing Orm. "I'll follow you."

Orm let out a yelp and raced away with his cloak flapping.

"Haakon," Kenna said quietly from behind him. "What is it?"

He turned. "I think King Athol is here. Astrid and Hamish are back and—"

"They are well?"

"Yes, yes, but I think they have seen him."

She swallowed, the sound loud in the quiet room. "They have *seen* King Athol?"

"Yes."

"Then we must prepare to fight and plan to win." Her fists tightened on the blanket she held around herself.

He strode up to her and cupped her face. "We will, my love. We will."

"Do you promise?"

"That is my solemn promise to you." He hoped to hell he could keep that promise. Keep his wife safe and defend the people of Tillicoulty he'd come to care for.

"Then I will hold you to it." She traced his lips with the tip of her finger. "King Haakon."

He stared into her eyes and fell even more in love with his wife.

He was a man of his word and a man of the sword. He'd die for love and he'd die for his gods.

But now…now he had too much to live for. He didn't see dying as an option.

Not yet.

About the Author

Based in the UK, Lily Harlem is an award-winning, *USA Today* bestselling author of sexy romance. She's a complete floozy when it comes to genres and pairings, writing saucy historical, heterosexual kink, gay paranormal, and everything in between. She's also very partial to a happily ever after.

If you're a Kindle Unlimited subscriber, you can read many of her books for free, including several complete series, and if you love sporty romances, get the first novel in her popular HOT ICE series when you sign up for her newsletter.

One thing you can be sure of, whatever book you pick up by Ms. Harlem, is it will be wildly romantic and deliciously sexy. Enjoy!

Website: www.lilyharlem.com
Amazon Author Page: author.to/LilyHarlem
Lily's Reader Group: facebook.com/groups/188731774881774

Find your next book boyfriend…
Male/Female
Male/Male
Historical Romance
Paranormal
Menage a Trois
Reverse Harem
Audio Books

For more deliciously steamy historical romance, including a plethora of stern Highlanders, dashing dukes, and kinky Vikings, visit Lily's website.

Made in the USA
Columbia, SC
07 April 2025